RIDE LIKE THE DEVIL!

Ben Trunch knew things were bad at home, and he retired from the Army because of it. He arrived back on the Big T only to learn that his father had shot himself. Trunch could see that a crafty piece of land-grabbing was in progress. He confronted Luke Fletcher, saloonkeeper and town boss, with what was happening, and was immediately forced to ride for his life. But he got the chance to put it all right in the end.

SAM GORT

RIDE LIKE THE DEVIL!

Complete and Unabridged

LINFORD
Leicester

First published in Great Britain in 1993 by
Robert Hale Limited
London

First Linford Edition
published 1997
by arrangement with
Robert Hale Limited
London

British Library CIP Data

Gort, Sam
  Ride like the devil!—Large print ed.—
Linford western library
  1. English fiction—20th century
  2. Large type books
  I. Title
823.9'14 [F]

ISBN 0–7089–5007–8

Published by
F. A. Thorpe (Publishing) Ltd.
Anstey, Leicestershire

Set by Words & Graphics Ltd.
Anstey, Leicestershire
Printed and bound in Great Britain by
T. J. Press (Padstow) Ltd., Padstow, Cornwall

This book is printed on acid-free paper

1

THERE it stood against the scarlet bars of the afterglow, centre of a black and sombre world that was familiar with seasons of a baking sun, times of blinding rain, and great winds that came whirling off the Gulf of Mexico and raised devils of dust along the crumbling edges of the plains. This indeed was the Big T ranch site — heart of the intended Trunch cattle empire! But if ever a dream had warped and twisted into travesty and illusion, it had happened here. So what had gone wrong with the once noble vision? If this wasn't the best ranching area in Texas, it was far from the worst, and men had already made their fortunes out of beef stock hereabouts.

Ben Trunch slowed his horse to a walk as he approached the ranch yard and continued studying what was left of his father's dream in this last hour of a dying summer's day. Judge not, that ye be not judged! Knowing of human frailty, no man could live by a safer rule than that, for the stuff of success as often came to a man with his blood as did the stuff of failure; and who was to judge of the battle — when one man fought the world and the other himself?

Shaking his head a trifle glumly, Trunch hoped there was an ultimate kindness behind it all. But he doubted it, and feared that he had let the conscience bred of his dawning maturity drive him into error. It had probably been a big mistake to throw up his Army career and return to this place on account of what Trooper Alf Wiseman had told him over in Fort Sumner, New Mexico. Just back off furlough, Wiseman had been full of his bad news and in no mood to spare his sergeant in the matter of what could be regarded as a son's failed duty.

It had been rubbed in that the

Big T was a rapidly declining ranch. Not that Trunch hadn't heard it all before, of course; but it seemed that things had gone from bad to worse with Trunch senior's lapse into drink and gambling. Wiseman had told Ben that Jack Trunch had borrowed heavily in order to bolster his situation with a lot of additional land and cattle, but had then been hit by the scourge of hoof-and-mouth disease. With nothing left to set against the interest on his debts, he had started gambling in an attempt to make the money that he had needed, but he had been out of luck there too. The word was that Jack was on his uppers and likely to lose everything before long. His health was also declining, due mainly to drink, and he hardly bothered to nourish or take care of himself any more. This latter factor, more than anything else, had decided Ben, near the end of his current five-year hitch with the Cavalry, not to sign on again but to come home and see what he could do about straightening things out. A man with any good in his heart couldn't just let a parent go to hell! But, the voice in his head now repeated, it had likewise been a sore and foolish thing to terminate a sound career, with promotion to sergeant major just around the corner, on account of another man's failure, father or not. Heaven knows! He had worked hard enough for what he had achieved! And now it was all gone — wiped out as result of a son's hours of pain and heart-searching. But he must not mourn the fact. There had to be more strength in him than that. He was a free man, and he had chosen freely. Now he must bear the consequences.

The rising night breeze murmured as Trunch reined in near the kitchen door, and a bat fluttered above his head. The dusk was heavy enough to feel in the shadow of the house, and Trunch's mount pricked up its ears as it started back just perceptibly in a warning sign that was characteristic of its training as a battle horse. "Cut it out, you damned old fool!" Trunch urged fondly. "There are no hostiles within two hundred miles of here. You're a civilian now, and you'll have to learn to behave like one!"

Yet Trunch wasn't too easy in mind about what had just occurred. He had seldom known the big gelding to be wrong when it had felt the need to alert him to something for which he ought to watch out. Perhaps Ernie Wheeler — his father's friend and constant companion from their mining years across in California — was lodged up in the barn or the stables with a rifle pointing at him. Well, Ernie knew his shape and could be relied upon not to press the trigger without cause, so Trunch let it go and dismounted, wondering rather absently why there was no lamp burning at this end of the ranch house while he had already seen one glowing behind the drapes at the parlour windows as he rode here along the trail from town.

Trunch walked up to the back door. He knocked firmly on the woodwork with the knuckles of his right hand. A good many seconds ticked away, and there was no hint of a response, so he rat-tatted again. Still no answer and, muttering to himself, he screwed round on the doorstep and called peremptorily: "Ernie! It's Ben! Are you up in the loft, you old sidewinder? Where the heck are you?"

He was almost certain that he would get his reply from the direction of the barn, but this was not the way of it; and he was distinctly surprised when his ears picked up a slow tread from within the house and the kitchen door opened to his again turning figure and he saw the pale-faced, balding Ernie Wheeler standing upon the threshold, eyes dull with misery, face collapsed into what looked like lined and leathery despair, and shoulders bowed beyond his sixty years.

"Hello, Ernie!" Trunch greeted jauntily. "You sure take your time now. Didn't you hear me knock the first time?"

"Oh, I heard you," Wheeler said shortly. "It seems like you haven't heard, Ben."

"Heard what?"

"You haven't heard," the older man said flatly. "Boy, folk don't gallop around in a house like this one."

"How's that?"

There in the gloom, Wheeler's face showed a conflict of emotions. "Blast it!"

Trunch had had a long, hard day in the saddle, and his anger blurted readily enough. "Have you gone and forgotten I used to live here? Aren't you going to invite me in?"

"What a homecoming for you!" Wheeler sighed, moving back and aside to let Trunch enter. "The pity's you haven't heard. I writ, y'know, but the letter must have missed you."

"I've left the Army," Trunch said in the smelly air of the kitchen. "It was a snap decision. Well, not quite,

I suppose. It was over at Fort Sumner. Alfie Wiseman came back off furlough and told me how things were here. You must recall Fred Wiseman's boy?" He sucked his teeth. "Yeah, your letter would have missed me."

"It was only writ two days ago."

"That makes it certain. I was on the trail then. Had been for a day or two."

"What'd you leave the Army for, boy?"

"To lend a hand here, dammit!"

"Nothing you can do here, Ben," Wheeler said unhappily. "Not now."

"To blazes with that!" Trunch exploded, fighting to keep a grip on himself. "Now don't make me riled, Ernie! You know what a bastard I can be when I get riled up!"

"You're a cough drop all right!" Wheeler acknowledged. "If only you'd called in somewhere in Miles Grove as you came through!"

"What is up here?" Trunch demanded angrily, shoving past the older man and stalking on across the darkened kitchen, his jaw turned across his left shoulder as he made for the light which showed down the edge of the cracked door that gave into the hall beyond. "G'dammit! I came straight through — wanted to get home!"

Wheeler moaned to himself, but spoke no word, and Trunch slammed on into the hall. He was desperately uneasy now, and felt an atmosphere in the house that he hadn't felt since ma's — Yes, this had to be death; he was suddenly sure of it. And he pushed through into the parlour and saw his worst fears confirmed; for there, standing on top of a pair of trestles, was a sealed coffin.

The shock was distinctly physical. It stopped Trunch in his tracks. He had come upon death many times in the last few years, but those deaths had not concerned him personally. This one was very much on the personal level, and meant the loss of his surviving parent. The anger had all drained out of him, and it was in the quietest of voices that he asked: "When did it happen?"

"Three days ago," Ernie Wheeler answered. "The funeral is tomorrow. I've arranged for him to be buried in the cemetery at Miles Grove. Around one o'clock. Perry, the undertaker, and his boys, will be along with the hearse about noon. I hope them arrangements suit, Ben, 'cos it's a bit late to change them."

"They're fine," Trunch returned. "How did my father die?"

"You don't want to know that, boy."

"Why not?"

Wheeler gestured helplessly.

"Get the lid off that box, Ernie!"

"Son," Wheeler pleaded, "you don't want to see!" Trunch scowled at the other. Then he went over to the lamp that stood on the sideboard to his right and turned it up to produce all the light he could get. After that he walked up to the coffin and saw that its lid had been only partially secured. One screw had been twisted down at head and foot, and one on either hand. Taking out his Cavalry jack-knife, Trunch opened the big blade and put its tip to work as a screwdriver. He twisted the screws out of their holes one after another, and soon all four lay together in his left-hand trouser-pocket.

"You don't want to see, Ben!" Wheeler now insisted, stepping up and placing a firm hand on the coffin's lid. "It ain't a pretty sight. I'm a-warning you!"

Trunch swept the older man's hand aside. Bending slightly, he lifted the lid away and stood it against the sideboard. Then he looked down on the body lying in the casket, blowing disgustedly at the faint odour of decay which had already started rising from the corpse. He forced himself to gaze long and steadily at his father, noting that Jack Trunch's face was horribly distorted and that the top of his head had been thickly bandaged. After that, swearing sulphurously, he swung away from the coffin and glared at Ernie Wheeler — though not so much in renewed anger with his companion as at the outraged state of his own feelings. "You were right, Ernie," he admitted. "It's nothing any son would want to see. God — what a sight! Did he shoot himself?"

"That's what he done, Ben."

"Ernie, I hoped he'd never do anything like that," Trunch said heavily. "Not that I'll have it's the coward's way out. No, sir! It takes a whole lot of courage to up with a pistol and scatter your own brains." He slapped fist and palm together, trying to understand. "I suppose it all got too much for him."

"No, Ben."

"Well, that's a — " Trunch began. "What do you mean: 'No, Ben'?"

"It didn't get too much. That's what I mean. It was made too much. He was driven to it."

"Okay, Ernie," Trunch said. "Explain it, that's all."

"Luke Fletcher driv him to it,"

Wheeler said, cowering perceptibly. "It was all calc'lated. Now don't you go and blow up, Ben!"

"I'm quiet, Ernie," Trunch assured him. "You've nothing to worry about now. I take it you're speaking of Luke Fletcher who owns the Tumbleweed saloon in Miles Grove?"

"Ain't no other Luke Fletcher what lends money and sucks the blood out of folk around here," Wheeler replied. "Your pa owed that buzzard a packet, and Luke and his lot encouraged Jack into gambling. He always prided himself on his poker face, didn't he? Anyhow, they slowly bled him dry!" Ernie wagged a cautionary finger. "I wasn't there, mind, that last evening, when Fletcher finally took the deed for this ranch off him. The story come to me secondhand, boy — from that barman, Joe Wones — but here's how it was told to Sheriff Carl Ives, by Matt Rakes, the dealer, when the lawman inquired into the matter after your pa had shot himself. If I can get it right."

"Just get the facts right," Trunch commanded.

"It appears to have been a poor evening in that back room at the Tumbleweed," Wheeler began, face all screwed up at the effort of it. "The cards had been comin' out all to hell. It seemed nobody had had a hand worth the mention. A real big pot had built up, and all of a sudden your pa come up with a just about unbeatable royal flush and figured that money for his. Except he got an unexpected challenge from Fletcher, and they went at it eyeball to eyeball and raised and raised each other — and your pa, like you can be sure was intended, finally got so het up and reckless he threw the deed for this ranch into the betting.

"Well, Ben, Fletcher showed. He'd got four aces and that beat your old man's royal flush, king high. It was a disaster pure and simple, and you might say Jack Trunch got no more'n he deserved; but what you've got to remember is old Jack's wonderful memory for cards. He swore one o' them aces had already been among the discards.

"Naturally, all present — being Fletcher's cronies and not your father's — reckoned Jack was mistaken and Luke had beat him fair and square. But Jack blew his stack and declared that Matt Rakes — the tinhorn I mentioned — had slipped Luke Fletcher that fourth ace under cover of lighting a cigarette for your pa. Seems there was one hell of a commotion after that, and Fletcher made a song and dance about your father being a poor loser — which Jack Trunch never was in all his days! Then, to shorten up that part of this here story, your old man was given a cut o' the skull by a bully boy and tossed out into the street.

"He rid home, Ben, and staggered in here. I could see somethin' was mighty wrong, but I knew better than to ask what. Next your pa carried a bottle of the raw stuff into his bedroom — him already being somewhat liquored up — and mebbe half an hour after that I heard his Colt bang. Well, I flew into his bedroom, and there he was — dead." Wheeler dry-washed his hands, sighing his despair. "That was that, Ben. You can't bring the dead back. No, sir! And that goes twice when they've scattered their brains all over the pillow and such. So I covered the body with a sheet, then rode into town and reported what had happened to Carl Ives. The sheriff sent me to the undertaker, then he walked across to the Tumbleweed and got the story I've just told you from Matt Rakes. It was confirmed o' course by the rest of Fletcher's gamblin' bunch. Ives was satisfied there was nothin' fishy in what he'd heard, and he rode out here next mornin' and advised me to go careful. Jack Trunch had been a troubled man — many knew that — and he had taken his own life. You can't blame nobody else for that — Ives said."

"Nor can you, Ernie," Ben admitted in a low voice. "He pulled the trigger himself."

"That he did, son," Wheeler affirmed. "You can't say other than that Franklyn Perry, the undertaker, did a fair job out here, even to fixin' up your pa's poor head. And, like I told you, there's the funeral tomorrow. Must say, I'm powerful glad you're here. It's like a miracle, Ben. Even if the circumstances are so bad."

Trunch gave his jaw an absent jerk. His mind had been no more than half on what was being said for the last several moments. There was an ultimate truth to be grasped, and he must grasp and accept it. "So this ranch is no longer the Trunch ranch, Ernie?"

"That's the size of it, Ben," Wheeler acknowledged sorrowfully. "The crew have all gone. There weren't above three boys left anyhow. I had just enough to pay 'em off, and they departed hat in hand, out of respect

17

for Jack Trunch."

"Nice gesture," the dead man's son reflected. "And well done, Ernie. When do we have to be out by?"

"Fletcher has given me until noon Saturday."

"The day after the funeral in other words," Trunch said ironically. "Big of him."

"He thinks so."

"Well, he can afford to be generous," Trunch observed. "I'd never have guessed he wanted this ranch that bad."

"He wants all the land he can get," Wheeler said. "He's out to put his brand on this corner o' Texas. There's big money in cows right now. Fletcher is out to make his fortune just how he can. He does a lot of his dirty work through that back room of his; but the greater part — so the whisper goes — is done through a gang o' rustlers he's runnin'. He's got big, Ben — and strong — and the folk around him have got correspondin'ly weak and small. There's no challenge to him. The risk's too big. What's worse, we're about as far from Washington D.C. as you can get down here — and we've yet to see the first o' them Federal Marshals ride by."

"I've heard that gripe in New Mexico," Trunch growled. "The people in this part of Texas pay as much in taxes as anybody else in this great sprawling country of ours. And it surely is a sprawl, man, when you take it from that north tip of Vermont right down here to Brownsville. Don't bear thinking about, old-timer, when you fork a horse, and I guess nobody gives a damn anyway."

"Not a damn!" Wheeler assured him bluntly. "Leave it at that, Ben. You always were a boy who wanted to right impossible wrongs. Your pa got a raw deal, and now you've got one because of it. But that's the way the cookie crumbles, son. There's still a lot more good about than bad. Just get on with your life. Try to forget what's lying there and what you've heard from me."

"I aim to," Trunch said with finality; and he went to the sideboard again, picked up the coffin lid, laid it back on top of his father's casket, and used his jack-knife once more as he replaced the four retaining screws. Then all was done, and he stepped back and added: "There you are, Ernie; that's it."

"Nice to hear. Just hold to it, Ben."

Trunch smiled faintly. He had the feeling that Ernie Wheeler didn't quite believe him. But he had accepted his father's suicide and felt no desire for revenge on those who could have caused it. He could still lose his temper, and fall into error as readily as anybody else, but he had also lived long enough to have found out that things that were not clear-cut were best left alone. While he was still ready to fight when he was sure of the right, his father's case was a dubious one, and only a fool made his life harder than it had to be in pursuit of the wrong. "This

I tell you, Ernie," he said on a sudden impulse of faith. "If Luke Fletcher is deep into wickedness, he'll be made to pay for it in the end. I've seen it lots of times already. The cleverest rogues only end up drawing enough rope to hang themselves."

"Does happen," Wheeler allowed, though he didn't sound entirely certain of it. "You look plumb tuckered. Want some grub? I've got some bread and bacon — sowbellies too."

"No, thank you," Trunch replied. "All this has crowned a real hard day, Ernie. My only need is sleep. Is my old room fit to use?"

"The bed ain't aired."

"That's another detail."

"Reckon you're a very fit man at that," Wheeler conceded. "Six feet three inches and two hundred pounds."

"Looks fine in a uniform," Trunch yawned, shrugging. "It's not much good on the range."

"A man can be too big all right,"

Wheeler said. "But yours is all bone and muscle. You're about right."

"Must be all that's right," Trunch commented, reaching out and patting the older man on his right shoulder. "If this has spoiled my life, it's ruined yours. What are you going to do now?"

"I can cook, Ben," Wheeler responded with a certain dignity. "There's always a place for a cook. We'll talk about it tomorrow, hey?"

Trunch flinched off a bleak smile. "Goodnight."

"Goodnight, Ben."

Trunch walked straight down the rest of the parlour and, coming to the door at the back of the room, opened it and stepped through into the corridor beyond. This gave access to the bedrooms, which were three in number — one on the right, one on the left, and one directly ahead. The room before him had been Trunch's sleeping place throughout his childhood, and he went to it now and entered, closing the door behind him at once and standing slightly sagged with his shoulder-blades resting against it.

Taking out a match, he struck it with a thumbnail. The flame burned dully in the room's dead atmosphere. He could smell unclean bedding and mildew in the walls. There had obviously been some very sloppy housekeeping around here in recent years, but he supposed that was almost to be expected of two ageing men without a woman between them. He guessed he could subdue his innate fastidiousness for tonight and perhaps tomorrow night as well. Yonder bed, with all its frowsy linen and faded coverlet, would be more comfortable to lie upon than many places that had received his soldierly head while out on patrol.

Going to the chest-of-drawers, he touched off the wick of the bedroom lamp and made the necessary adjustments to produce the best light. After that he kicked off his boots and removed his gunbelt, slinging the latter over the back of a cane-bottomed chair. Then, deciding that he might as well sleep on top of the bed — and with his clothes on — he threw himself down on the coverlet and stretched hard, relaxing an inch at a time until he was totally limp.

Now the full force of his situation hit him. His intended act of self-sacrifice had come too late; he would be burying his father tomorrow. He had left the Army, and this, his home and expected inheritance, was now the property of Luke Fletcher. He had no place to go, and must start over again. There wasn't one redeeming aspect to what had happened. He had money enough for a few weeks, but knew he would have to give Ernie Wheeler something to be going on with — which meant that he would have to find work even sooner than he had at first expected. But what could he do? And who would have him? He disliked cowboying, and had no trade or manual skills. So what did that leave him? Only hunting or guard work of some kind. He ought to have left the Army years ago — when he was most needed here — or, better, never joined it in the first place. The small virtue of his years had been literally squandered. If he had been a selfish young shaver, today had certainly paid him out as nothing else could. He lay bereft, thinking on a suit of black storeboughts and a decent pair of boots for the funeral tomorrow. To such fell uses —

He drifted a bit, fighting to make the best of it, and was getting close to sleep, when he was shocked fully awake by the sound of a rifle going off not too far away. Heart thumping in his chest, he sat up and listened intently, and he heard Ernie Wheeler — at the further end of the house — open the kitchen door and step outside. After that came minutes of breathless hush, but there was no further explosion and the tension gradually decreased. Then Trunch heard Wheeler re-enter the house and lock up behind him.

Finally the other man came padding exhaustedly through the parlour and into the passage outside the listener's room. "Ernie!" Trunch called.

"Going to bed," the other answered.

"What was that shot?"

"Can't say for sure," Wheeler returned indifferently. "There's a fox about. It's been killing hens at Norton's farm over yonder."

"Ike Norton, eh?"

"He's been out at night several times lately, trying to put paid to that varmint with his gun."

"So what have you been doing?"

"Stablin' your horse, Ben. Did you aim to leave the critter standing at the rail all night?"

"Thanks, Ernie. I'd forgotten him, and that's a fact. Though he's not used to being pampered."

"Daresay he likes to sleep comfortable when he can."

"Yeah," Trunch chuckled. "That shot was nothing?"

"I'd say not," Wheeler answered, his

voice stretching as if afflicted by a big yawn. "Goodnight — for the second time."

Grinning mechanically, Trunch shut his eyes again. He trusted Ernie, and Ernie had been satisfied that the shot had been nothing to worry about; so he wasn't going to worry. But there remained a quiver in his nerves; and he was still a mite uneasy all the same.

2

IT was a peculiar sensation, and not
one that Trunch had experienced
too many times in his life. It
was that of coming awake abruptly
and realizing that he had overslept.
To an Army man that represented a
shameful breach of discipline, and he
swung himself off the bed and stood
up sharply, shaking all over. What
would they say in the guardhouse?
After this his name would be a by-
word for slackness and irresponsibility.
The captain might even have his stripes
for it!

But then, in the broad daylight, he
saw the peeling and battered furniture
of his grubby little bedroom about
him, and the feeling of mortification
dropped away from him. Of course,
it didn't matter any more; he could
sleep all day if he wished. Footloose

and fancy free, he was a civilian. He was also a man with little to hope for and a funeral to attend. There was responsibility left, dammit! He ought to have been up and doing hours ago! There were those duds to buy, a haircut to get, and an Army draft on the bank to cash. He also hoped to see a few familiar faces around town. A guy could never quite shake off his fond feelings for his school pals.

The lamp still burning on the chest-of-drawers called his attention, as did the apparition in the mirror on the latter's top. He was indeed an unshaven and rumpled mess, and guessed he stank a little too. Blowing out the lamp, he told himself that a man couldn't ride all those hundreds of miles from Fort Sumner without a bath and not smell of his horse and his own sweat. He needed a good hot tub, but he guessed he'd be lucky on this ranch.

Rasping at his chin, Trunch went sockfoot to the washstand; but, as he

29

had feared would prove the case, found no water in the jug. Showing his teeth, he managed a grin; it was no good getting irritable about it. Last night he had entered upon a bad job, and he could only keep it tolerable if he went looking for Ernie Wheeler with a pleasant expression on his jib and kindly feelings in his heart. Ernie had never done him anything but good, and deserved good in return. It would be fine if they could part on a kindly word and a warm handshake.

Trunch stamped into his riding boots. Then he left his bedroom, walked down the passage beyond, traversed the parlour — ignoring his father's coffin en route — and entered the kitchen, where he found Ernie Wheeler brewing coffee and toasting bread. "What have you got?" he asked.

"Bacon and beans."

"You did say."

"No miracles overnight, son."

The back door was open and,

smiling, Trunch passed on into the yard. Here he stopped beside the pump and, bending at the waist, made to douse his head thoroughly with cold water; but he had yet to crank the handle when Ernie Wheeler stepped out of the house and began walking towards the eastern edge of the ranch site. "Where are you going, mister?" Trunch said curiously.

"Just want to see."

"What's there to see?"

"If it's still there."

"If *what's* still there?" Trunch stressed exasperatedly.

"I saw a horse standing over the way earlier," Wheeler now explained in a much louder voice as he raised his left hand to his eyes and peered across the land. "It's still there."

"That's remarkable for these parts?" Trunch queried ironically. "I thought the redcoats were coming!"

"It ain't so funny."

"No?"

"Come and see."

Yawning widely as he swept the fingers of his left hand through his thick brown hair, Trunch ambled to where the older man was standing and took up position beside him, following a digit that pointed across country.

"See it?" Ernie demanded.

"I see it," Trunch answered, concentrating on the black animal about a mile away and deciding that he couldn't see it well enough. "It's a saddlehorse."

"It's standing on the trail," Wheeler mused. "I wonder who owns it? I can't see hide nor hair of its master. Can you?"

"No," Trunch responded, a hint of disquiet stirring in him. "You put my horse up last night. Did you leave my gear with it?"

"Just as you packed it, Ben. I took your stuff off your mount and stood it to one side. But nothing more."

Trunch nodded, and turned away. "Going to get my field-glasses." Slanting to his right, he soon entered the nearby stables, going immediately to the stall in which his gelding stood. He saw his saddle on the partition adjacent and his bags standing beneath it.

Unstrapping the more worn of the two saddlebags, Trunch rummaged out his field-glasses. Then he walked back outside and returned to where Ernie Wheeler occupied the same position as before. "Have you seen anything different?"

"No."

Putting the field-glasses to his eyes, Trunch screwed in the focus, bringing the black horse across the range into clear and detailed magnification. The creature appeared a fine mount, and was undoubtedly tricked out in the best of accoutrement, but of its rider there was definitely no sign — though the hang of the brute's reins suggested that the man had jumped down and parted from it hurriedly.

There was a rock-pile to the left of the trail and not far from the horse. Trunch shifted his lenses towards the heaped boulders. Now he glimpsed a pair of small shapes jutting above the grass at the base of the mass. Those objects could well be a man's booted feet. Fractionally adjusting his field of vision, Trunch peered through his field-glasses more intently still — recalling the rifle shot which he had heard the night before — and he soon became sure that he was indeed looking at a pair of boots with toes upturned. "Ernie," he said, "I believe there's a man lying in the grass at the foot of those rocks. If that isn't the soles of a pair of boots pointing this way, I'll eat my hat!"

"Well, let a man have a look then," Wheeler said, reaching up for the field-glasses.

Trunch let the other take the binoculars from his grasp. Folding his arms, he stood by while Wheeler put the glasses to his eyes and made one or two clumsy adjustments, sniffing and swearing between times. "I can't see no boots," he complained.

"Maybe you need specs, old-timer," Trunch suggested, reclaiming the field-glasses. "Anyhow I'm going to take my horse and ride over there. Unless I miss my guess, there's something sadly amiss over yonder."

"Never rains but it pours!" Wheeler observed. "Still, you and your pa were always a pair for talking trouble up!"

"Speak no ill of the dead, Ernie," Trunch advised sternly. "Or was it all aimed at the living?"

"You bet it was!" Wheeler agreed fervently.

Trunch laughed shortly. Then he jog-trotted back into the stables. Here he put his field-glasses into the top of the bag from which he had recently taken them and buckled up again. After that he quickly saddled his horse, backed it out into the yard, and stepped astride, lifting a hand to Wheeler as he spurred clear of the ranch site and picked up the town trail on the land beyond, working his mount to a gallop in the first twenty yards and holding it flat out as they moved into the big left-hand curve of the trail and approached the spot where the black horse was now stirring at the sound of hooves. Nearing the animal, Trunch lifted in his stirrups and immediately confirmed that there was indeed a man lying at the foot of the rock-pile on the black's left, and that the other lay ominously still.

Halting his own mount just short of the black, Trunch sprang out of leather and ran over to the supine figure under the boulders, kneeling in mid-stride to end up at the man's side. The other's fine-boned, aquiline face, grey as winter, was not unknown to him, and he frowned at the downed body as he sought swiftly for a pulse or any other trace of life; but the man lying there was dead and had probably been so all night, for the large circle of blood on the front of his lawn shirt was completely dry and already a trifle faded. "Caught up with you, has it, Matt?" Trunch gritted, jacking himself back to the vertical and standing over the corpse; for the dead man was that same Matt Rakes, the dealer at the Tumbleweed saloon, who had probably played such a crucial role in the run up to Jack Trunch's suicide. "What the deuce were you doing on the Big T? Suffering a slight attack of conscience maybe?"

Trunch walked over to the black horse. He led the animal up close to the body. Then he wiped his hands down the sides of his yellow-striped Cavalry trousers and braced himself. After that he picked up the gambler's remains and threw them across the back of the mount that he had just stood in position. Now he went to his own horse and obtained a rope from his second saddlebag. Then he returned to the corpse and tied it in place without more ado. Thinking was all very well, but it got nothing done by itself. The body belonged in town, and the reasons for Rakes's death were the sheriff's business. Feeling balky, he was of the mind to go on right away — and to hell with everything! — but he threw off the worst of his resentful mood and, leading the burdened black up to his own horse, remounted and began drawing the gambler's animal after him in the direction of the ranch house. He must tidy himself up a bit, and he couldn't leave Ernie Wheeler high and dry. The old-timer had the right to know what was happening.

The trot back to the ranch yard took minutes longer than Trunch's headlong gallop to where the gambler's body had lain, and he was able to watch Ernie moving about the space impatiently throughout his approach. "Who is it?" Wheeler shouted, while the incoming man was still almost a quarter of a mile away.

"It's Matt Rakes," Trunch responded, but only when he was close enough for Ernie to see for himself. "He's been shot. I reckon somebody stood on those rocks over there and put one into him from almost point-blank range. Figure it was that shot we heard last night."

"Murder? Somebody was laying for him, Ben?"

"I don't see how else to read it, Ernie."

"Oh, by gosh — by golly!" Wheeler breathed. "Why?"

"An attack of conscience perhaps?" Trunch queried, dismounting. "I always got on well enough with Matt Rakes. He was Luke Fletcher's man, yes; but there was good in him. It's likely he'd seen me ride through Miles Grove earlier on and wanted a word with me before we slept."

"That could have been regarded as treacherous, Ben."

"In certain quarters — it would have been."

"So a bushwhacker was sent out ahead to cut him down in the dark?"

"Adds — give or take a detail."

"What are you going to do with the body?"

"That should be obvious, Ernie. Take it to Sheriff Ives."

"Ain't there a risk there? I mean,

Ives knows we had no cause to love the hellion."

"Now you have put me off my breakfast!" Trunch declared, his brow beetling, for Wheeler had just indicated an aspect of this matter which had not yet occurred to him. "Carl Ives couldn't believe such a thing!"

"Why not?" the older man inquired. "There's a slug in that dead man, and who's to say in what circumstances it got there? The need for revenge can boil up a man's brains! You'd motive enough to kill that gambler, and who's to say you didn't — me? That's none too believable either!"

"We're looking on the black side, Ernie!" Trunch protested. "Whatever's there has got to be faced. I see no cause for you and me to jeopardise our futures with any jiggery-pokery whatsoever." He rasped at the stubble on his chin again. "I need a scrape; then I'm off to town. I've other things to do there besides this."

"You can drink a mug of coffee and

stuff a round of toast down your throat — while you shave."

"Didn't I say? I'm off my breakfast."

"What kind of soldier are you?"

That one made Trunch pull a face; but there was no answer to it that wasn't quarrelsome. So he went dipping into his saddlebags again and spent a minute locating his shaving things. Then, with his razor case, lather mug and soap in hand, he walked back into the kitchen, Wheeler moving at his heels and muttering repeatedly.

A large, smoke-blackened kettle stood steaming on the hob. Trunch picked it up and carried it to the sink. There he poured a small amount of boiling water into a tin bowl, laid out his tackle, and prepared himself for shaving. After that he went to work with his cut-throat razor and soon removed the considerable growth of beard which had hidden his good looks up to now. Then he combed his hair and slicked it down with some water, and finally he gave his boots a polish by rubbing each leather top against the calf of his opposite trouser-leg. "You wouldn't pass the captain's inspection on parade," the watching Wheeler announced, "but I reckon you'll do for these parts. Where's your pistol?"

"I left it in my bedroom."

"Go and get it."

"Ride into town looking like some damned gunfighter?" Trunch wondered. "No. There's a Winchester on my saddle if I do need a gun. Anyhow, it might prove wiser to enter town looking harmless."

"You must know," Wheeler said shortly.

Trunch wasn't altogether sure that he did know, but did have certain instincts — and he felt that he should follow them when he could — acknowledging that, in a general kind of way, size alone kept a fellow safe. True, gunpowder mocked muscle, but you could safely travel the middle path most of the time, since folk who were looking for the kind of trouble which killed were not that numerous. "I'll hope to be back in a couple of hours, Ernie," he said. "You may depend on it that I'll be here when Franklyn Perry drives up with his hearse."

"Righto, Ben," Wheeler said. "Don't worry about your shaving things. I'll clear up after you. Git, boy!"

Offering a word of thanks, Trunch stepped back outside and returned to his horse. Swinging up again, he took Rakes's corpse-burdened black in tow once more and trotted that animal and his own out to the town trail, heading for Miles Grove now at an even pace and expecting to cover the rather less than four miles between the Big T and town in something over the half hour.

He rode with head bowed. The passing scene was summer-brown and open, and he paid little attention to it, since he was full of uneasiness again. His immediate future contained uncertainties that he could not ignore, and there was so much of a practical nature to engage his mind beyond that. There was, too, an undoubted grief present — and the lingering sense of guilt as to how he had failed his father. Not that the latter emotion was in any degree disabling, since there was too much innate fatalism in him for that; but, while he believed that life would always develop as it must, he was also certain that right thinking and doing could modify events and sweeten relationships. His trouble, he had to admit to himself, was that he had too often ignored the needs of other people in favour of what was best for him. He guessed this fault made him no worse than the majority of folk that he had known, but that wasn't much of a comfort this morning. Ben Trunch was being forced to learn about Ben Trunch, and the lesson was mainly wormwood and gall. Even if the present events helped him to be kinder and more understanding in the future, nothing could alter the past. And you couldn't say sorry to the dead. If 'sorry' wasn't far too convenient a word anyway.

Before long he came to the dirt hill which sheltered Miles Grove from the great winds of the south. Passing over the eminence, he gazed down into the somewhat hollowed land beneath. Miles Grove was a pretty place. A row of great cedars — unusual for Texas, and particularly this part — ran down its eastern flank. On the other side of town, a flashing silver presence amidst the shadows of its willows and cottonwoods, a watercourse meandered. There were corn and cotton fields in the offing too, and the scattered farm buildings of the outskirts had a roseate glow upon their rooftops about now. Trunch, as often in the past, couldn't see the town developing into one of importance — because it served no real commercial purpose in the neighbourhood — but it was a centre of population and that was sufficient for the day.

Yet, despite the foregoing, the main

street was busy enough as Trunch rode off the northern face of the hill and entered it. There were waggons around, shoppers on the boardwalks, horses standing outside the saloons, a coloured sweeper on the church steps, and a Butterfield stage leaving for Corpus Christi as another rolled in from San Antonio. Fashion had also come to this butt end of Texas, Trunch reflected, as he passed the milliner's window, where French ribbons and English laces were on display. But then his thoughts were rudely interrupted as a very large man stepped off the sidewalk to his left and stayed his progress with a particularly heavy hand that came down hard on his thigh. "Hold it right there, Sergeant Trunch!" came the command.

"Yeah, it's me, Carl," Trunch agreed, looking down and giving Sheriff Ives a bleak grin. "You don't have to get formal. I'm still Ben, and a civilian now. I just happened to muster out in this Cavalry shirt and pants."

"Do you care what I call you?" Carl Ives asked. "Ben Trunch. One of our bad pennies turned up again, eh? Well, soldier or civilian, what's that you've brought in? I can see it's Matt Rakes's black horse."

"Bearing the body of Matt Rakes," Trunch said, feeling slightly nettled by the giant lawman's hectoring manner — "as I think you can very well see."

"Yeah — I got good eyes."

"I found Matt earlier this morning — dead — on the trail and about a mile from our ranch house, near that last pile of rocks on the way in. Looks like murder to me — though you'll decide that, of course."

Ives went to the body and inspected it — or as nearly as he could manage to, allowing that the corpse was quite closely bound to the black horse's back. "Who did it, Ben?"

"Haven't a notion, Sheriff."

"Nor much else by the look of you," Ives said, his voice filled with a needling significance which matched

47

the probing stare of his grey eyes and the tightness in the lines that further disfigured his seemingly adze-hewn features. "At that, I was sorry about your pa. It must have been a shock for you."

"I didn't know about it until I got home last night. Ernie Wheeler told me about it then."

"When your pa got into playing cards, he would plunge."

"I know that, Sheriff."

"Ernie would have stirred it," Ives calculated. "This isn't your work, Ben? Did you shoot Rakes?"

"I did not!" Trunch flamed. "And may you rot in hell for asking it!"

Ives wagged a cautionary finger at him. "I am the sheriff, and I have to ask — and don't you ever speak to me like that again!"

"You were suggesting I'd given way to revenge," Trunch said grimly, not one whit abashed.

"Over that fourth ace, yes."

"Might as well have it clear."

"You're sensible enough."

"That's what I want you to accept!" Trunch insisted. "Carl, I wasn't there. I wasn't in Fletcher's back room. I don't know what happened. I've only heard Ernie's version of it, and that was secondhand. I'm not prepared to judge. There's a whole case and months of doing involved. My father must have been up to his eyes in debt!"

"Okay," the lawman temporised. "Just you keep thinking like that. But about Rakes. You don't know who shot him, but you must have some thoughts on how he came to die. Well?"

"All right," Trunch said flatly. "This is pure speculation, Ives. Figures Rakes either saw me pass through town on my way home last evening, or heard about it. I think he was riding out to the Big T for a talk with me when he was gunned down in the dark. You don't have to be all that clever to work out that he probably wanted to talk to me about what had happened to my father in Fletcher's gambling den over at the Tumbleweed. Thanks to what Rakes may have done, my father had lost everything — for me, too, as his heir — and it's possible Matt wanted to communicate something to help me set the matter straight."

"Maybe. He could have been plain scared of you."

"If he'd been that, Sheriff, he'd have run."

"How about if he meant you violence?"

"I knew Matt Rakes a little years ago," Trunch said soberly. "Matt was probably a crooked gambler from time to time — but he was no backshooter."

"He's still dead, and we still need his killer's name."

"Somebody knew he'd left town for the Big T — and why. That has to be the answer, Sheriff; and who could that have mattered to but Luke Fletcher? Right?"

"Wrong as can be," another voice broke in, speaking mildly and yet with a certain authority; and then a large, fleshy man stepped from the shadows of a nearby doorway and crossed the sidewalk to stand beside the lawman. "It sounds to me like I have an interest in this matter, Sheriff, and I'm going to say once and for all that a few obvious facts are being made to fit a generally lying theory. Ben Trunch is the man at risk — not I."

Trunch gazed coldly at the speaker, taking in the other's firm round face, too-straight eye, gleaming pomade, and tailored posturing. "Come off your high horse, Luke!" Trunch advised. "I've said nothing behind your back that I won't happily say again to your face. As for the rest, I'm glad you've come sneaking up. This does concern you, and you might as well be here first as last!"

3

THE sheriff was in all respects the man between, and Trunch saw that the lawman looked rather uncomfortable. Indeed, Carl Ives was visibly forced to subdue a strong reaction to the antagonism which was evident between the ex-sergeant and the saloonkeeper. "You might have held your noise, Luke," he said mildly. "I had everything well in hand. Nevertheless, Ben Trunch is right. You are involved, and you might as well be in from the start." He tucked his thumbs into the top of his gunbelt. "You've said Trunch is wrong, Luke. I'm asking how so?"

"I saw Ben ride through the main street last evening," Fletcher explained, "and it was I who called Matt Rakes to me and sent him out to the Big T." He shook his head, apparently much bewildered by the surprise which his statement had evinced from the other two men. "For heaven's sake! What's so strange about that? I realized how Ben would naturally feel about the Big T having become mine, and I wanted him to hear my true account of what had happened in my back room as opposed to the mess of lies that I knew Ernie Wheeler was going to feed him. Ernie wasn't present at that last game, but Matt was. Anyhow, once the talking was over out there, I'd asked Matt to tell Ben that I'd like to see him next morning — that would be this morning — here in town. I hoped I'd be able to round off any doubts left outstanding and settle this whole sorry affair without too much bad feeling."

Trunch raised his eyes to heaven, pleading. "Bad feeling!" he choked out, almost at a loss for words amidst his cynical laughter. "When were you ever an honest man, Luke, much less a saint?"

"When was I ever in trouble with the

law, Ben?" the saloonkeeper inquired, eyes dirty but pitching it low. "Carl?"

"He's as clean as a whistle, Trunch," the sheriff confirmed. "I've never had to put a black mark against his name."

"We've all gone raving mad!" Trunch announced bitterly. "Can you see the rot at an apple's core?"

Apparently stricken by a sad helplessness, Fletcher sighed and shook his head at the sheriff. "See what we're up against, Carl?"

"Look here, Ben," the sheriff said sternly. "We're all mighty sorry about your dad, but you have no right to go pitching into an innocent man."

The words were a form of catalyst and they brought Trunch's true feelings bursting through the last of his attempted moderation. "Innocent man! I'd stake my life he's as guilty as sin!"

"Ben, you could be doing that!" Ives warned. "You always did have a big mouth, and the Army's made it even bigger! I've heard an argument from you, sure; but I need some material evidence. Show me some proof of what you've said. Can you do that?"

Trunch could not. He could only draw himself erect in the saddle and sit tight-lipped.

"He sits accused by his own silence," Fletcher said in mingled sorrow and disgust. "That's what you get for exercising good nature with a hothead, Carl. I was bent on keeping it friendly — still am." He showed his hands in mute appeal; then, in the tones of one making a last great effort, he went on: "Ben, your father called the tune. All I did was play out my clearly winning cards against his. It wasn't my fault that I couldn't lose. Other men who were present will tell you the same."

Though inwardly certain that he was the man in the right, Trunch felt the saloonkeeper's spurious story pushing him further and further into the apparent wrong. A number of townspeople had now formed a knot close to what was going on, and he could see from their faces that Fletcher was carrying the day and any more accusing words from him would only be regarded as the final justification for whatever retaliatory action he brought upon himself from the law or Fletcher's direction.

"Well?" Sheriff Ives demanded, seeming to have sensed the ex-sergeant's more cautious frame of mind. "Can you fault the reasonableness of what Mr Fletcher has said? I've given you every chance; more than I ought to have done."

Mouth crimped, Trunch just couldn't bring himself to shake his head. With all his inner conviction, he felt demeaned, dented in pride, and reduced in dignity. The onlookers clearly saw him as a man of low character and no honour; and, what was worse, he detected an evil glint in Fletcher's eyes that said the saloonkeeper was going to take full advantage of his humiliation.

"Ben, I'm not a man to hold a grudge!" Fletcher declared, sounding hugely gracious about it. "I remain prepared to do all that I had in mind at first. You've lost your inheritance, and that's hard. But life's hard, and we have to learn to accept it as it comes. Now, if there's anything you want to take away from your ranch house — when you leave the Big T this weekend — you have my full permission to make whatever arrangements you want to do just that. Can I speak fairer?"

"Sounds real generous to me, Trunch," the sheriff commented, his words raising a mutter of agreement among the onlookers. "Mr Fletcher is just about falling over himself to be kind."

"All I'm determined to have is the land, stock, and buildings," the saloonkeeper added. "Now let's hear no more about it. Be a man, Ben, and come and have a drink with me."

"You do that, Trunch!" the sheriff advised, taking the black horse's reins out of the ex-sergeant's hand. "I'll take Matt Rakes's body to the coffin shop."

"I've got a funeral later on," Trunch said reluctantly, "and I must buy some things to wear for it."

"You've got time to go and have that drink with Luke Fletcher," Ives said, at his sternest and most compelling again.

"I don't think so," Trunch returned.

"Shame!" cried one of the watchers; and somebody else let out a hiss.

Trunch was suddenly conscious that this could turn ugly in a general sense. He clearly didn't have much support over there, and there were those among the townspeople who didn't mind making trouble. It wasn't worth allowing his pride to push this folly to the limit. He must demean himself a trifle further and choose the lesser of the two evils. "All right," he said. "I'll have that drink with Fletcher."

Nodding his grim approval, the sheriff walked away with the black horse, while Fletcher, beckoning to the ex-sergeant, left the sidewalk and slanted across the street, heading for his property, the big and garish Tumbleweed saloon. Entering the place without looking back, he left Trunch to ride after him, dismount, tie up at the rail, dust off, and then pass through the still gently flapping swing-doors and into the low-beamed but reaching gloom of the bar-room.

Easing at the top of his trousers, Trunch glanced around him. The faces of the customers told that they had been aware of what was going on outside, and that they now wanted to see what he would do next. Then a number of other men — no doubt with the same idea in mind — pushed in from the street and Trunch was borne up to the divide by their advancing presence whether he liked it or not.

He halted beside Luke Fletcher, who was now leaning against the bar, a bottle of bourbon in one hand and a pair of glasses in the other. The saloonkeeper set the glasses down on top of the carved woodwork and began to pour. He filled both almost to the brim, then put the bottle aside and raised his own glass in salute. Forcing himself to it, Trunch did the same, though he was aware in the same moment that the atmosphere was suddenly filled with hostility towards him. This, then, had been anticipated, and it appeared that he had walked into a trap. He had realized that Fletcher was putting on an act out in the street, but he had not quite twigged that the man meant him immediate harm. There was a set up here, and this was abruptly proved when a tall man, hard of body and wide of shoulder, but very lean, shot to his feet at the back of the room, his scarred face snake-eyed and accusing, and said: "I'm Ray Porlee, Trunch, and I carry the fastest gun there is. Matt Rakes was my friend. We know you killed him. Nobody else could have done!"

"Nicely, Mr Fletcher!" Trunch rasped. "Got me by the short and curlies, haven't you? You had Rakes killed sure enough. But you're afraid of me — that's what this here charade is about! Now that's a caution, isn't it, because I was prepared to let it all go and ride away? You must have come near fouling your britches when you saw me riding by last evening. It's all been a rare old coincidence, Luke; but, yes, things do indeed happen like that!"

Fletcher shot back his drink, while Trunch carefully set his down again. "I don't know what you're talking about, Ben," the saloonkeeper said evenly. "Why, you're worse than Bill Cody for tall tales. Good job I know how it is with you, isn't it?"

"You've played me pretty neatly," Trunch admitted, "and that's a fact. You've also got that great lump of a sheriff on the same hook."

"Nicely put, Ben!" a woman's voice called from the opposite end of the bar. "Our Luke is a master fisherman!"

Trunch glanced round quickly, smiling in some surprise at the female — a firm-lipped, russet-haired woman of around thirty, who combined a faintly world-weary expression with the bold eye of a free-liver — and he exclaimed: "Why, Sheila! It's been a few years, girl! You on another of Luke's hooks?"

"Still," she agreed.

"Wicked waste!" Trunch opined.

"I squandered a bit of time on you too, as I remember, you big rat!" the woman countered, bringing a cold smile to Fletcher's face as he poured himself a second bourbon.

"You certainly have been generous with those charms of yours, Sheila Wilson," Trunch acknowledged humorously. "How does Luke feel about it? I can't say you look a mite the worse for it. You've hardly aged a day since that time you and I went walking down by the lily pond. Or did we walk that day? It was hot, honey, and I figure we laid around some!"

"I'll tell you this, Benjamin!" Sheila Wilson replied. "You were no gentleman back then, and you certainly haven't turned into one since you joined the Cavalry."

"Be that as it may," Trunch said, "you'll always be lady enough for me."

"Bless your cotton socks, boy!"

"All right, Sheila," Luke Fletcher said in a voice which was low and harsh, "that's enough!"

The woman nodded, and turned to her left, facing the door just beyond the end of the bar which gave access to the saloonkeeper's private rooms. "So long, Ben."

"See you in hell, Sheila!"

She gave a little nod, then withdrew, leaving the door slightly ajar behind her.

Now Fletcher made a sign to the still erect Ray Porlee, who, in his turn, gestured to a group of men sitting at a table near his own. The men, four in number, rose instantly, and the biggest of them, a bearded hook-nose with red-rimmed eyes, cast a noosed rope over the beam that crossed the middle of the room and gave support to three hanging lamps. The other three men — of the same villainous cut as hook-nose — began slowly threading the tables about the floor in the ex-sergeant's direction, and Trunch raised an eyebrow at Luke Fletcher and said: "Going to have a private hanging, are we?"

"That's the size of it," the saloonkeeper agreed evilly. "The town will see the need for it — after we've put it round how you confessed to murdering Matt Rakes."

Trunch picked up his glass of bourbon again — then shot it straight into Fletcher's eyes; and the saloon-keeper reeled backwards, covering his face and crying out in pain. But he did no more than grunt as Trunch hooked him with a terrific left and he fell into a heap.

Conscious that it was now or never, Trunch sprang into the air, bounced off the fallen man's midriff and sailed over the bar — landing in the well behind it and thus avoiding the body of the room and the hands that were already darting at him — and after that he dived for the wicket in the woodwork opposite and shoved through it, crabbing swiftly to the right and then passing through the door which Sheila Wilson had left ajar on leaving the bar-room.

Now he found himself in a passage that was short and narrow. He saw the woman at the other end of it. She was standing in a room which he took to be Fletcher's parlour. Sheila Wilson's handsome face wore a look of deep anxiety, and she used both hands to beckon at him with the greatest vigour. "Run, Ben!" she softly encouraged, turning to her right as she spoke and vanishing behind a papered corner of the room which jutted there.

Trunch reached the spot from which the female had vanished. Feeling a draught from the left, he turned in the direction that she had gone. Before him he saw a back door standing open, while in the yard beyond it a strawberry roan mare stood unattended and ready for riding, its neck slightly bowed. Trunch ran outside, his soles just touching the ground, and vaulted onto the mount's back, spearing the stirrups and grabbing back the reins with the sure actions of a man who had virtually lived in the saddle since his earliest years. Then, throwing the swiftest of glances about him — seeking a glimpse of the saloon woman, of whom he had seen nothing more — he struck with his heels and loosed out, hearing Sheila's voice from somewhere nearby call in tones low and strong: "Ride like the devil!"

The exhortation inspired. Trunch sent the strawberry mare lunging across the saloon's back yard. Ahead of him he saw a five-barred gate in the fence behind the stables. Lifting the brute, he jumped it cleanly over the barrier and brought it down safely on the thick grass of the meadow beyond. There was a sudden outbreak of firing in his wake. The shots crackled and popped, and he thought he heard a bullet pass his right ear, but no slug touched him or the horse and they sped on across the land.

Trunch saw before him now that green line of vegetation which marked the presence of the watercourse on the town's northern flank. Ducking low, he let the horse plough through the veil of low-hanging foliage without much loss of momentum and bound off the bank onto the hard, pebble-strewn floor of the shallow stream beyond, splash onwards for a few yards more, then scramble up the opposite shore and stretch into the country of the main ranching outfits hereabouts.

Up a moderate slope Trunch pounded now, climbing steadily for the next half a mile and coming to where the greener pastures about the stream's course degenerated into the coarse tussocks of the already summer-browned prairie. Here the distance hung, powder-blue and cloudless, and the dim traceries of a further dimension told of the hills along the Neuces river and the watersheds of the southeastern plains. It was all vast and appealing to the eye, but at this time Trunch found its magnificence dismaying, for it seemed to him that there was just the scene and that all concealing detail was lost in its spread.

Sufficiently raised to look back and down into Miles Grove, Trunch turned his head and peered hard for a moment or two. What he saw made him curse under his breath. Luke Fletcher's people had already managed to mount up and were now galloping after him. He had hoped to be able to cross the brow of the land before those fellows could begin the inevitable chase, but they now had him spotted up here and would be able to form a clear idea of the direction in which he was headed. Pushing his mount to the limit, he balanced himself as nicely as he could and thought hard. Not for an instant did he doubt his ability to elude his hunters, for nobody knew these parts better than he — since he had played over all this land during his childhood and knew its every secret — but he didn't want to half kill the horse that he was forking. He realized that it must be Sheila Wilson's personal mount and used to nothing more than a woman's gentle exercise.

But, leaving all the clever stuff aside, he was in no mood for riding rings around those guys behind him. He had had scare enough in the Tumbleweed saloon and just wanted to get away from Miles Grove and go where the hell he pleased afterwards. He knew what he needed to do — had done ever since fleeing Fletcher's place — and his chief regret was that it seemed he would be required to pull out all the stops when he had expected his final escape to be so much easier.

Yet what must be must be. He hardened his mind. He would give his hunters the same run-around that he had given Billy Gibson's son, Adam, about fifteen years ago. Adam, that great bullying lummox, had been going to beat him to a pulp after an argument at school, but Ben, ever fleet of foot, had got to his pony ahead of the other's swinging fists and galloped into the countryside, bringing Adam after him on that mule which Gibson had given his son to ride.

Ben had led Adam across the stickiest of the Drago swale — almost causing him to bog down — and then he had moved on and entered the brush due south of here. After that he had diverted out of the thickets, at a spot where no diversion appeared to exist, and emerged on his father's own land from between a pair of grass hills that were known locally as the Twins. This latter action had, so Trunch had learned the next day, lured Adam into the brush and got him so thoroughly lost that he had been found howling for his mama. It had been the sort of triumph which had fixed the oversized Adam the way that the Adam Gibsons of this world should be fixed. Getting lost in the Texas brush was a sobering experience for anybody — especially as there were still a few rogue bulls left in there from the days of the longhorn herds — and, while Trunch hardly expected to reduce his pursuers to despair, he imagined that he might be able to give them something to think about for an hour or two.

He eased up a trifle on his mount. Great haste was not vital to his plan at this stage. Despite his recent misgivings, he did in fact have a big lead over the men who were chasing him, and his success depended on their keeping him in sight for the time being. If he caused them to fall back too far, he could fail to lead them into the mire. Besides, he owed it to Sheila Wilson to make the best of his opportunity, for he suspected that she had known what was to happen to him and left her horse saddled and ready for his escape from the yard. The woman might be required to answer to Luke Fletcher for what she had done; and, while he didn't doubt that she would manage to talk her way out of her 'carelessness', her risk should not go unappreciated. Even if she had tried to protect Fletcher from himself by this morning's act, what she had done was still immensely to her credit, and Trunch marvelled — not for the first time — how women of her dubious morals could so often turn out to be far more caring than their stainless sisters.

Aware that he was already on Gibson land, Trunch kept an eye out for cattle and Broken G riders, but he saw neither. He had this quarter of the pastures to himself, and that was just how he wanted it, for he wished to begin his shift southwards without needing to worry about anything more damaging to his scheme and concentration than gopher holes or any blemishes that might emerge in his memory of the route.

Soon he found himself riding parallel with a prairie ridge which was formed of brown banks and limestone outcrops. Moving in closer to the rise, he watched the ground begin settling before him. This was the path down into the swale. He could already see the greener places of the low, where deep springs kept forcing moisture upwards even in the hottest of the weather and a certain amount of swampiness was obviously present.

Trunch moved deeper into the swampy basin, keeping as close to the base of the ridge as his horse could get. He recalled that a narrow strip of land along the foot of the climb on his right had always been perfectly firm. But it wasn't long before he perceived that the going today along this favoured strip was far from perfect. Indeed, the lowest ground of the hollow was trodden into mud and water where many beeves had pitted the swale with their hooves while entering an arched tunnel which Trunch knew to pass clear under the ridge and provide access to a hidden meadowland in further sunken places on the opposite side of the prairie crest.

Wondering why Billy Gibson would be driving cattle under the ridge these days — since Wolf Bottoms, as the hidden pasture was known, had always been regarded as too inaccessible for normal working — Trunch felt the irritation of being unexpectedly slowed right down to a walk and forced to pick a careful path across the churned up area. The task quickly absorbed all his attention, but he soon cleared the danger area and reached firm going again.

Now he looked back across the swale, knowing that he had lost a lot of ground to his pursuers — who were already galloping within gunshot of him — but this worried him much less than the fact that glimpsing his difficulties had warned the riders behind him not to follow his tracks anywhere near exactly, and the horsemen were now steering for firmer land out to the left where the depression was also less acute. These manoeuvres should enable the hunters to come level with the position that he had now reached in about a third of the time it had taken him to cross the worst of the boggy hole. And that done, closing the gap still more on equal terms might not prove beyond them, since it was evident that one or two of the men back there were even better mounted than he.

All at once things didn't look too favourable. Up to this moment Trunch hadn't worried too much about his lack of a gun, but now he wished he had a rifle. Given a Winchester and a good eye, the fugitive could always slow up his hunters with a few accurate shots, but as of this time he was at the mercy of any pursuer who hauled off and set up his sights for a bout of steady shooting. He was not yet of the mind to kill anybody, but it would have been nice to be able to discourage those who wished to kill him. When all was said and done, there was no great crime about cutting the horses out from beneath hunters who were getting too close. He had done it often enough when fighting Indians.

Turning his eyes to the front, Trunch gave all his attention to riding again, forcing the strawberry mare to stay at the limit now. For all his apprehension, no shots were fired as he angled across the path of the men in his wake, and presently he saw the brush ahead of him. A mixture of blackthorn, mesquite and brambles — with a leavening of cacti and garlands of Spanish moss — the tangle looked a vicious eyesore to be avoided at all costs; but, lacking the protection of chaps and gauntlets, Trunch spurred straight into it, suspecting that his pursuers imagined him to be trapping himself in the process.

Wincing at the inevitable rips and tears that came his way, Trunch didn't shirk his need and kept driving onwards. He picked up a natural path within the thicket, and let this lead him to others which were distinguishable from the rest of this jungle only by his memory of where they led. In fact he persisted with his heart pounding in his throat, for he knew that the years could radically change even established patterns of growth, but the matrixes that he sought seemed much as before and he kept slanting southwards and eventually dived into what looked by far the densest and least penetrable of the spiky quadrants.

Checking amidst a maze of thorn and beanwood, Trunch cocked an ear and listened in the direction from which he had come. It seemed to him that he heard a mutter of sound from back there, but after that there was silence. Pretty sure that his hunters had already lost track of him, he let the strawberry mare go on at the walk — regretting the bloody mess that it, like himself, had become — and he soon picked up the first of the landmarks which he sought in this direction.

It took the form of a wild cherry tree that was gnarled with age, shedding its bark, and alive only here and there.

Branching left into the thorny shrubs on the left of the tree, he soon came to a pile of white rocks which emerged like a huge, sugar-topped pudding from amidst a big clump of Spanish Dagger. This pointed him to a small clearing where the bleached skeleton of a catamount had lain crumbling for a generation — and this in its turn indicated a thicket of live-oak which was girdled by daunting walls of yucca.

Guiding his horse to the left-hand corner of the live-oak, Trunch drew a deep breath and dismounted. It was going to make things tricky if the years had choked the next stage of his escape route with cacti or some growth equally resistant. But he'd soon know how the matter stood when he forced back the shrub which concealed the head of the narrow way which should lie there. The tall bush was still growing just as he remembered it, and everything about it looked much the same also. With a little luck, his progress should continue.

The signs were improving again.

Easing his right arm into the dense foliage of the all-important shrub, Trunch located the bole at the centre of the growth and steadied himself against it for a moment. Then he threw his weight sideways and the tall bush bent away from him, revealing a kind of path to its rear — which was in fact, as Trunch perceived for the first time, a partially surfaced ridge of flint that showed above the red shale of the area. It appeared anything but a way to safety, but the sight of it filled the fugitive with pure relief and he knew that he was virtually home and dry.

Stepping further still into the shrub, Trunch drew his horse into the gap that he had made and eased it past him. After that he moved forward and round to his right, allowing the bush to resume its original position in full and cover the start of the narrows behind it. Remaining afoot — and facing his animal in order to lead it directly over extended reins — Trunch backed along the flint ridge, negotiating further thickets by this means and putting up a few sagehens as he emerged from the densest of the growth where a number of old cattle paths converged. Facing round again, into a somewhat changed scene — with juniper and greasewood clothing many of the coarsely grassed bumps and banks of the land before him — he made out the prairie edge at a distance of half a mile and, mounting up, rode towards it now, finally breasting out of laurel and green willow onto the feed-grass itself.

Stirring the strawberry mare to a trot, Trunch gazed back into the brush, smiling thinly as he pictured the probable discomforts that were being suffered by the pursuers who had now quite obviously lost him completely, and then he looked to the front once more, clapped on further speed, and rode out between the two grass hills known as the Twins onto what had been the most northerly edge of his father's Big T range.

Galloping for home, Trunch shielded his eyes from the fiery south, where summer burned along the far hills of the Rio Grande and a haze danced upon the nearer grasslands under a sun approaching the zenith. It was all so familiar, and it brought back the memories of childhood. But where had the herds gone, and what had become of the men who had worked them? This once teeming grass was a brown desert now — a desolation restored to the silence of a million forgotten yesterdays. Often, in his early nightmares, he had feared that his home would disappear and he would be orphaned off the range. Well, if that hadn't occurred, literally, it had happened near enough. He was riding where he no longer had a right, and the Trunch name was no more. For the first time he felt the hand of rejection hovering over him, but he was determined that he would not be finally swatted.

The ranch house came into view

across the land. He no longer wished to go there, but he knew he must. For had he not promised to see his father's coffin off the premises? His mind had recently been everywhere but here, and he wondered if it had been a form of instinct that had delivered him at the last. Yet what came next? Something had to come next. Was he still going to ride south? Only God knew!

He was approaching the ranch yard almost before he was aware of it. The hearse was already there, its figured glass sides full of the sun but its glossy black team equally dulled by the dust. Franklyn Perry was standing on the other side of the beasts. He looked impatient to be getting on with the funeral. Doubtless the man had a grave-digger kicking his heels back at Boot Hill on twelve cents an hour. Expenditure of that magnitude made a true businessman want to get a grave filled in as quickly as possible. Well, that would not worry the late Jack Trunch any, and it was no worry to the dead man's son either. The sooner the body was removed, the better for everybody.

Trunch reined in opposite the kitchen door. The entrance stood open, and Ernie Wheeler was poised upon the threshold. The man saw him, but offered no acknowledgment of his presence. Trunch was vaguely disquietened by that — annoyed too — and he felt a warning shiver in his spine; but he decided that this physical reaction could be explained by the sudden appearance, at the front corner of the house before him, of four black-suited men carrying his father's coffin towards the waiting hearse.

Then, not totally to his surprise, a man holding a gun emerged from that same forward corner of the dwelling, three others stepped out from behind corners of the barn and stables, and Luke Fletcher straightened into view from a place of hiding near the back of the hearse itself and pointed a revolver at him. "Get your hands in the air,

Trunch!" the saloonkeeper ordered, a ring of triumph in his voice. "I thought you'd come back here!"

Trunch began to lift his hands. Now he came to consider it, he supposed the likelihood of his return to the Big T ranch house had been quite obvious. If he had misled the men sent out to hunt him, he had allowed himself to fall into error still more foolishly. Often it was the deepest thinker who missed the obvious!

4

TRUNCH'S hands had reached no more than the height of his shoulders when Ernie Wheeler moved. The ageing man stepped out of the kitchen doorway, right hand clawing underneath the hem at the back of his jacket, and he jerked a pistol from the rear of his waistband. Then, swiftly reversing the weapon in his grasp, he threw it to Trunch, who took it out of the air in the knowledge that it was his own Army Model Colt forty-five and as reliable a gun as the entire country could supply.

At that instant Luke Fletcher dived along the further side of the hearse and reappeared behind the black horses of its team. This brought him opposite Trunch and within six yards of Ernie Wheeler. Fletcher fired straight at the old-timer, and Wheeler staggered. "Get

85

the hell out of here, Ben!" he gasped, then fell onto his face and kicked abruptly onto his back, shuddering into total stillness.

You couldn't mistake death, and for a split second Trunch was horrified; but he didn't let the shock paralyse him and, as Fletcher ducked from view, matched shots with the man who had originally stepped out from behind the forward corner at this nearer end of the ranch house. The bullet fired at him missed by the proverbial whisker, but his own slug pierced the centre of his adversary's chest and wrote an immediate finish to the exchange.

Fire flashed and powder roared from Fletcher's direction. Hot lead plucked at Trunch's right eyebrow. He blazed in reply, but the chuck of his frightened horse sent the shot well wide and into lancing contact with the haunch of the further wheeler on the hearse. The animal neighed shrilly, kicked up — almost jumping the traces — and banged down again, its fear already infecting the rest of the team; and off went the black brutes, towing the hearse behind them, and the bearers were left stranded with the coffin still resting on their shoulders.

Exposed by the glass-sided vehicle's abrupt departure, Fletcher went sidling to his right, triggering at Trunch as he moved, and Trunch snapped a return from a twisted position in his saddle and raised blood on his enemy's left cheek. Crying out in pain, Fletcher reversed course instantly and concealed himself behind the bearers — a coward's course if ever there was one — and, mocking the saloonkeeper with both sneer and curse, Trunch yanked his horse about and fired at a man who had advanced from the nearer western corner of the barn in an effort to shorten the range and get off a certain shot. The oncoming figure took a solid hit, reeled back against the timber wall of the building behind him, and slipped to the ground, sitting there with his chin rolled into the hollow of his left shoulder as if asleep.

Trunch's pistol dared the next man to show himself. Two shots spat at him from the further corner at the front of the barn. One bullet clipped the seam of his shirt under the left armpit, and the other plucked hair from his horse's mane. Shrinking back from the near misses, Trunch could hardly believe his luck when the gunhand from town suddenly dived out of cover — apparently to see to the man whom the ex-sergeant had previously shot at the other side of the building — and Trunch aimed and fired, again scoring a perfect hit and dropping his man on the spot.

Despite the clear sky and brightness of the sun, an atmosphere of horror settled darkly over the ranch yard. Too much death had come too suddenly to the place. Then the minds present — at least those on Luke Fletcher's side — seemed unable to accept the tragedy and violence of it all any longer, and somebody shouted for a retreat and the sound of running feet became audible behind the stables. Bawling his fury, Fletcher lumbered after his withdrawing hirelings, a fist waving in the air as he ran out of the kind of words that a gentleman would never have spoken.

Filled with the devilish exhilaration of success, Trunch felt inclined to launch out and pursue his demoralised foes, but he realized that he had done well enough and forced himself back under control. Calming, he held his horse down and looked towards the funeral party, two of whom were standing over the lowered coffin while the other two were running in pursuit of the bolted hearse. Clearly he could provide no help there and, throwing Ernie Wheeler's body a last sad glance, Trunch pointed his mount in the direction from which he had recently come and spurred back into motion, thundering northwards at a pace which would hardly make pursuit worthwhile if his foes from town should recover their courage and decide that they wished to give battle another whirl.

Thrusting his revolver into the top of his trousers, Trunch asked himself once more what on earth he was doing? He could only find another heap of trouble in the direction that he was now riding — yet there was a resolve in him now which had not been there before. If he had been unsure that he had a cause to start with, he was convinced that he had one now. Luke Fletcher's behaviour had already confirmed that he had cheated Jack Trunch out of the Big T, and his efforts to kill Trunch's son and heir could not go unchallenged. The fear of Ben that Fletcher had betrayed must be visited upon him in full. Yet the irony of it remained that, in twice attempting his murder, Fletcher had brought upon his own head the very trouble that Ben Trunch had been prepared to leave alone in the first place. The saloonkeeper could actually have enjoyed the fruits of his latest crime with no comeback; but now, though Trunch had little idea as yet how it was to be achieved, he was going to end up with his criminal world in ruins and the hangman's noose dangling above his head. For the cold-blooded murder of Ernie Wheeler was one that was not going to go unpunished. If Trunch had to open the trap under Fletcher himself, the saloonkeeper was going to pay in full for that crime. Short of judicial hanging, a bullet would have to do the job; but whatever happened Luke Fletcher was going to die. Trunch's mind was set, and his determination just as awful!

Toying with ways and means — especially as he examined again those other vague details which he had received from Ernie Wheeler last evening concerning the scope of Fletcher's illegal doings — Trunch came again to the two grass hills known as the Twins and passed between them, reentering the brush shortly afterwards. What with the rustling and other ranch dispossessions in the neighbourhood, it occurred to Trunch, as the live-oak and cacti sprang up about him again, that Fletcher must have made many enemies and that there would be a lot of folk around who would gladly provide all sorts of information that could harm him; and he was wondering if there would be any future in seeking to contact Sheila Wilson again and asking her to be his ally against the saloonkeeper, when a male voice hailed him from the top of a nearby thorn tree and advised him to halt. Reining in, since he had detected no recognisable threat in the tones from above, Trunch called back: "Who are you? What do you want?"

"I'm just adding ditto to that!" the other answered.

"Won't you come down and show your face?" Trunch inquired. "I favour leaving the trees to the birds!"

"That sounds like Ben Trunch sure enough."

"Right on the nail!"

"This is Charlie Stokes."

"Oh — ah!" Trunch thought a moment. "The Charlie Stokes who owns the Rafter S?"

"The Charlie Stokes who used to own the Rafter S," came the slightly mournful response; and this was followed by scrambling noises and some shuddering and shaking of the branches as a body descended the thorn tree.

Frowning, Trunch pursed his lips and held his noise. He thought he'd let Stokes join him before he had anything further to say. Now the man dropped out of the tree and, long, slim and fortyish, walked over to the rider, shoulders hunched, hands in pockets, and a Winchester tucked under his right arm. "Hello, Ben," he said, all ears and nostrils as he glanced up, a brown eye narrowed in a shrewd and questioning manner. "I heard shooting from over your way not long ago. Did it have anything to do with you?"

"Everything. You alone?"

Stokes jerked his chin across his left

shoulder. "I have friends back there."

"Doing what?"

"That's where we live."

"Where you live?"

"Out of Luke Fletcher's way — but not too far."

"You're watching him? That man's a polecat!"

"Did he have to do with that shooting?"

"Uh, huh."

"Welcome back to these parts," Stokes said dryly.

"Luke just said it," Trunch tempered sourly.

"From what I've heard," Stokes went on, "it's been gathering for you. But how the deuce did you manage to tumble into that load of horse apple so fast?"

"Pure coincidence, Charlie. I arrived home at the wrong hour on the wrong day."

"As I live and breathe!"

"So long as Luke doesn't do that too much longer!"

"He has fixed ways. He robbed your papa much as he robbed me."

"I'd like to hear about it some time."

"Anybody hurt over there?"

"I think four men are dead. Only one mattered."

Stokes pursed his lips in a silent whistle and looked grave. "Who was that?"

"Ernie Wheeler." Trunch quickly told how the gun battle had come about, ending: "Fletcher and his bunch had me cold in the ranch yard. Ernie tossed me a gun. Luke shot the old guy down like a dog."

"I see how it was," Stokes said. "Well, you always were better than handy with a gun."

"It was part of the reason I joined the Army, Charlie."

"As a matter of fact, Ben, I did see you ride through here a while ago."

"Like I told you, coming from the Broken G direction."

Stokes frowned at his toes. "Billy

Gibson is thick with Luke Fletcher. I'd put him down as the only friend Fletch has got locally."

"You don't say?"

"That's the trouble, I do. Yet there's no more to be made of it — that I know."

"You've got serious rustling hereabouts, haven't you?" Trunch queried, his mind quickening.

"Yes," Stokes replied, "and I'm sure Fletcher is behind it; but you won't catch him riding the night himself. It's our guess Ray Porlee is paid to do that for him. The herds left around here are being steadily bled, and those thieves leave the occasional dead man behind them to discourage any nightherders who might be out to make a name for themselves. Porlee is a wicked hellion — double-dyed, I might tell you! He made things too hot for him up in Kansas, and I reckon that's why he came down here and tied in with Fletcher."

"You've got to know a heap more

about all that than I do," Trunch observed. "Would I be right in thinking you could be looking for a cow cache?"

"That's a fair enough deduction," Stokes acknowledged. "Those stolen beeves are being held someplace until they can be fed into herds going north."

"With their brands blotted."

"Betcha," Stokes said narrowly. "What's this leading up to?"

"I've got an idea that might be worth following up."

"Cow cache?"

Lifting his jaw, Trunch slowly let it fall.

"It's possible me and my friends could have missed something, Ben — but I doubt it."

"It's just that I'd pit my knowledge of these twenty square miles or so against just about any man's."

"Yes, you were always a fair ranger as a kid," Stokes remembered. "I was that ten years on from you. I used to envy you, Ben — did you know that?

Your pa mostly. He let you be a boy. My pa always told me, if our ranch was to be mine, I'd got to work for it from beginning to end. He was a hard man, old Cyril Stokes."

"My old man was no bad father at that," Trunch agreed. "He gave me all the rein I needed. There were some bastards about at that time of day. They never should have had kids."

"Well, my pa was no businessman really," Stokes said reminiscently. "He sold to the government, when he should have put his beef on the open market. Then there were bad investments. You put those things with tic fever — he borrowed a packet off Luke Fletcher just like your pa did. Fletch forced me to sell all, just to pay the interest owing — and then my missus went and died. Dammit, Ben — sorry! I didn't mean to bend your ear with my troubles!"

"It's all right, Charlie," Trunch comforted. "It was too bad about your wife. I liked her well."

"Everybody did." Stokes smiled.

"Where do you think that cow cache could be then?"

"You must have heard of Wolf Bottoms."

"Sure," Stokes drawled. "But they're deep in Gibson land. And the approaches to them, the Drago swale, can be a death trap when we get a real rain up from the Gulf. I don't think Wolf Bottoms have ever been seriously grazed."

"But they're there," Trunch insisted, "and I rode past the way into them not three hours ago. That wet place had been trampled into maggoty cheese by cows."

"Recently?"

"Very, I'd say."

Stokes made a circle of his lips and blew hard through them. "I can't just ignore this — and I'm sure my friends will feel the same. Going to take us there?"

"You know the way as well as I, Charlie," Trunch responded. "Nor do you need me to find a path for you across these thickets, I'll be bound."

"No," Stokes agreed. "The security this place gives is mainly due to the fact that we know the brush through and through. Not that we've given Luke Fletcher — or anybody else — a reason for hunting us as yet. There's game enough around. Water, too, if you know where to look for it."

"I do know. But it appears to me you haven't got far with what you're doing up to now."

"I guess not," Stokes admitted flatly. "We need clear evidence of crime against Fletcher. Most of what he does is too clever to take him into court. Look at how he took our pa's. The average judge would be more inclined to blame them than Fletch." He breathed in deeply, considering Trunch with a frank eye. "Ben, you're a natural leader. Do you want in, boy?"

"I have to rest my head somewhere," Trunch commented, "and playing a lone hand does have its disadvantages.

But if there's a chain of command, I'm not going to horn in."

"We need somebody with a military turn of mind."

"I was only a sergeant."

"No 'only' about it!" Stokes snorted. "A man's got to be a cut above average to get three stripes sewn on his sleeve."

Trunch nodded judiciously. "Okay, Charlie," he said, "I'm in. If I seem uncertain, I guess it's because it's all happening so fast."

"I reckon," Stokes allowed. "So you're out of the Cavalry?"

"I am."

"Their loss is our gain — for now. Because I swear you'll be going back in." Stokes spat dispassionately. "Oh, the harm these family loyalties do to the man."

Trunch sighed. He had reached the stage where he was beginning to think in those terms himself. After all, he had done himself nothing but harm and everybody else no good. Yet he wasn't an old man, and his actions of recent weeks could still be written off to experience. With all the loss of pride and other things that it could cost him, he might even now do what Charlie Stokes expected. "Whatever," he remarked, more to himself than the other. "There's plenty that needs doing here before I'm likely to see Fort Sumner again. What have you got to show me, mister?"

Turning to his right, Stokes said: "Climb down and walk it, Ben."

Trunch dismounted. Going to the red mare's head, he drew the brute into Stokes's wake. They left the through path and entered choked gardens of thorn and Spanish Dagger. Often they snaked where no track seemed to be, and a few minutes later they arrived in a small, boulder-ringed hollow. This had a spring at its centre and a picket line at its back. In between the water supply and the tethering spot, two tents of weathered canvas had been erected. A smokeless campfire was present too, and six men of widely differing ages rose from about it to greet the incomers — if with a wary interest in Trunch and hands resting on the butts of their revolvers. "What's this, Charlie?" the oldest man present asked, an aggressive tilt to a large face that was heavily fringed with a white beard and topped a square-shouldered body which had a chunky stance. "Company?"

"You know who it is, Askew," Stokes returned. "You saw the young devil grow up, and he's still got the same ugly mug he always had. It's Ben Trunch — Jack's son."

"Hello, Ben," Jonathan Askew, once of the Circle A, greeted, offering a hand. "We got a warble from a sagehen, a while back, which said there was somebody floating around."

"Interesting bird," Trunch commented, shaking the proffered hand and feeling the firmness of its grip. "You a victim too?"

"He means of Luke Fletcher," Stokes said helpfully.

"Luke diverted the water away from my range when he took Charlie's Rafter S," Askew explained. "In that respect, I suppose I was on sufferance from the first, Ben. But it was always live and let live with the Stokes family."

"It sure is a catalogue up against Fletcher," Trunch observed. "That rattlesnake should be glad of the law that keeps watch over his hole. In the old days of not so long ago, a man who attempted to treat his neighbour the way that varmint does would have been run out of the district on a rail!"

"That he would," Askew agreed, grimacing resignedly. "We're enjoying the benefits of law and civilisation, eh? Only a crook can use them best. Good men make it easy for the bad. Sometimes I ask if beneath it all they want to." He gestured dismissively. "Mysteries from the book of hell, son. You'd better meet these fellows, then have some grub and coffee."

Trunch gave Stokes a sharp glance of inquiry.

"Hey, up, Askew!" Stokes checked. "This man's arrival is business first and everything else a long last. He's got an idea where Fletch may have his cow cache. I think we should go and check it out right away. I know Ben does too."

"Sure do," Trunch agreed. "This isn't something we can do by night."

"Where do you reckon it is then?" Askew inquired.

"Wolf Bottoms," Stokes shot in. "On Billy Gibson's Broken G."

"Heard of them," Askew said. "Never been there."

"Near the Drago swale, dad," added a perceptibly greying man, in early middle age, who was of Askew's own cut.

"No good repeating myself," Askew said, shrugging. "You'll remember my sons, Ben." He pointed to the one who had just spoken. "Sam." Then he nodded at two other thick-set men, who were younger than the first by a number of years but of the same strong Askew body and features. "Tony and Jim."

"Fellows," Trunch acknowledged. "I remember Tony and Jim from school. I reckon Sam — like Charlie Stokes — was bearing the heat and burden of the day when us kids were learning our lessons."

"We don't all enter this life together," Stokes said shortly, "and that's a fact. While we're at it, the other two guys are Bob Median — who ranched that corner of grass out at Low's Creek — and my own boy, Frank Stokes. He's just turned twenty, Ben, and makes you look an old man."

"Between 'em," Trunch returned dryly, "the Army and the Apache managed that years ago. Hello, Frank."

"Mister Trunch."

"I'm not that old!" Trunch protested. "Pluck up your courage, Frank!"

"Whatever you say, Ben," Frank Stokes replied, a rosier and heavier make of man than his father, though no less tall and of the same strong bone structure. "You aim to lead us onto the Gibson ranch. Ain't that trespassing?"

"It sure is," Trunch agreed, "and correspondingly dangerous. But I don't figure you men have gathered here because you're desirous of living to be ninety."

"You can say that again, Trunch!" the rather Latin-looking Bob Median almost snarled. "We haven't a future worth a damn between the lot of us. Our only ambition is to see Luke Fletcher dead and buried. Oh, hasten the day!"

"Wait along," Trunch counselled. "Life just doesn't stop like that — unless we stop with it. You'll come through this okay, and pick up again on the other side. Now — your horses yonder look as if they could do with some exercise, and so do you."

"Well?" Stokes queried, when a moment of hesitation ensued.

Median picked up the coffee pot.

He extinguished the campfire with its contents. Then he and his companions went to the picket line. Trunch hung lightly on his mount's jaw and watched them untying their horses. After that, their mounts caught at the bit, the ex-cattlemen began walking back across the low. Charlie Stokes was in the lead and, slotting in behind the man, Trunch moved out of the basin as one of the party.

Still afoot, they set off into the brush on the north of the low, following a newly trampled path into an area where a broader and natural track allowed them to mount up and stir their horses to a trot. Now they made real progress, touching a few of the spots that Trunch had himself traversed earlier on, and presently they emerged from the thickets on the pastures opposite the sunken land which contained the Drago swale.

Realizing that they might have the need to dissolve back into the brush hurriedly, the riders checked while still close to the thickets. The members of the party rose in their stirrups almost as one and looked around them, but this part of the Gibson range was just as deserted as Trunch had found it that morning. With everybody settled back into leather, Stokes got the party moving again and the men rode across the open grass and came to the western edge of the marshy valley in the plain. Settling under the rim, for the concealment of the land, they turned northwards again and galloped over the side of the slope above the wet place until it brought them to the southern face of the ridge that contained the tunnel which gave access to Wolf Bottoms. "Better stick as close to the foot of the rise as you can, men!" Trunch cautioned. "It's sticky enough there, but it's a heck of a lot worse further into the low!"

Stokes hung back, signalling for Trunch to pass him. "Okay, Ben," he said, "it's your show from here on."

"Right," Trunch answered without

hesitation; and he led on down to the valley floor and the quagmire which bordered the entrance to the tunnel in the base of the rise adjacent.

Holding a light rein, Trunch attempted nothing fancy or rash. For the most part he controlled his mount with his knees and was content just to keep it moving. The animal negotiated the hoof-broken surface of the valley mud without much difficulty and answered the bit readily enough as he turned it into the tunnel. Ducking low to avoid the massive slab of limestone which tilted above him to form the roof of the passage, Trunch waited until he was sure that he had solid ground beneath him and then dismounted. He went to his mount's head again and, feeling a leader's natural concern for the men behind him, he was tempted to remain still and wait for the rest of them to join him under the ridge, but he realized that his companions were competent men and had no need of his supervision. They could safely be left to shift for themselves, and would come on fast enough, remembering that this kind of snooping could finish in a pile of trouble and there was every need for haste.

Trunch looked along the tunnel. He could see the light at the end of it. From his childhood experience he recalled that the passage was without pitfalls and he could move along it as quickly as he liked. He stepped out confidently in that knowledge — promptly opening a gap between him and his nearest follower — and he was through the tunnel and standing in its egress before anybody else began to follow him directly.

It was still full day, but Trunch found himself in the shadows on the further side of the ridge. Hardly bothering to glance into the golden blaze of light at the back of the sunken meadowland before him, he remounted and kneed his horse forward again. He became aware of a few knots of cattle ahead of him, and was filled with satisfaction at the sight, when his horse snuffled a warning and caused him to raise his eyes and gaze beyond the cows. Now he saw four horsemen galloping towards him. The riders had their pistols drawn, and they were coming at him like informed men with a deadly purpose. It figured, then, that he and his companions had been spotted on their way here — probably from the top of the ridge — and that the fellows charging him now had ridden down into Wolf Bottoms, by some route known to them, with just this attack in mind.

Feeling that it was vital his friends in the tunnel should be warned of what was happening out here and given the chance to back off and escape, he turned his head and yelled at the top of his voice: "Back! — back! Go on back and run for it!"

Then he drew the Colt from his waistband and went charging at the men who were bearing down on him.

5

TRUNCH passed out of the shadows and into the glare of the sun. He perceived at once that the gap between him and the riders converging on him was closing faster than he had believed possible. He could already see the faces of his four enemies clearly and, although each had markedly different features, the message stamped on their lineaments was the same. These men knew no fear and had little mercy in their natures. They had been bred hard and were born to kill; no argument on earth would turn them from their ways. It looked like kill or be killed. Yet where was that so different? He had fought many battles with the Apache, and each had carried the same stricture.

The guns opposite started banging. As bullets whipped past him, Trunch watched smoke jet from the weapons pointed at him and whisk away. Thumbing at the hammer of his own Colt, he aimed at his nearest attacker — who was bearing in upon him from the right — and squeezed the trigger. He received an instant impression of his slug lacerating the near side of the charging mount's neck, and the creature chucked away from its injury and danced wildly, providing its rider with a fight to control it.

Cocking his gun again, Trunch saw that the man at whom he had just fired and missed was now an easy mark on his prancing horse, and he lined his sights once more, determined to make a job of it this time, but his hammer fell on a fired shell and he realized, besides lacking the means to make a reload, he had given no thought to the almost empty state of his Colt since his fight with Luke Fletcher and company. Furious with himself — since he could undoubtedly have obtained some ammunition from Charlie Stokes or one of the other men back there — Trunch hurled his sixgun with all his strength at a rider who was trying to blast him out of the saddle from well inside throwing distance to his left, and he had the slight satisfaction of seeing the heavy pistol strike his man full in the chest and send him reeling out of his saddle; but his pleasure in this success was instantly nullified as he perceived that his first enemy had now fully lost out in his attempt to control the injured mount that he was forking and that the maddened brute had just come bucking back directly into his path.

Sensing disaster, Trunch did everything in his power to turn his own horse away from the other; but the red mare was unable to check fast enough and drove headlong into the hurt animal before it. Virtually unprepared for the violence of the impact, Trunch felt himself lifted out of leather as if he weighed little more than a feather, and his body jerked and snapped upwards to a height of a dozen feet and more — rolling over and over as it crossed the zenith of its rise — then down he plunged and struck the ground several yards beyond the point of collision. The impact was a frightful one, and his brain burned like scarlet coals fanned by the bellows — though the vivid light died instantly into the impenetrable emptiness of a black midnight.

For a long time there was nothing and, when at last Trunch did start regaining consciousness, it came to him that his previous state could be the proof that there was no life beyond this one, for nothing could have been more dead than he had seemed to be. Then the pain hit him, and for long moments he could comprehend almost nothing but its presence. He groaned, as agony encapsulated the core of his skull and, eyes fast shut, reckoned the only treatment must be to stand up and try to shake his suffering away. To this end he first attempted to sit up, but a pair of hands that were firm if gentle came to rest on his shoulders and forced him flat again, bringing the awareness that he was lying on a bed and had a cold compress on his forehead.

Now Trunch opened his eyes. The glow around him was that of lamplight. Within it everything lost form and swam. Using his will instinctively, he fought the particles in the streams of radiance, and the scene gradually reassembled about him. He discerned a ceiling that was crossed by beams above him, papered walls on either hand, drapes closed at the window, a chest-of-drawers, washstand, and the tall brass rails at the foot of the bed on which he was resting. Then he turned his head to the right, causing the compress to slide off his brow, and muttered to himself: "What's life worth?"

"Whatever it means to you," a young woman's voice answered, not unkindly. "Keep still, Ben! I think you must have come very close to breaking your neck.

117

I have heard that your head is too thick to ever take much harm!"

"Thank you," Trunch said, making out the speaker standing beside him — a quite lovely dark-haired girl, with lustrous eyes that were large and rather sadly appealing in the pale oval of her face. "Thank you kindly."

"I aim to please, sir."

"Do you, by damn!" he snorted, nevertheless feeling a lot better for the sight of her. "Who are you that knows me? You don't look old enough to have been more than a child when I was at the age you're at now."

"That covers it exactly," she agreed. "I'm Janet Gibson."

"Janet Gibson?" Trunch pondered, making quite an effort of it, for his brainpan still seemed to be full of scrambled matter. "Yeah, that's right. Billy Gibson had a daughter — that brute Adam's sister — a little mite who was all pigtails and calico britches."

"The pigtails I've trained otherwise," the girl responded, "but calico feels too uncomfortable on a woman grown."

"It doesn't look up to much either," Trunch confided. "Am I in the Broken G ranch house?"

"Yes."

"Am I a prisoner?"

"I fear you are."

"So those men I fought over at Wolf Bottoms brought me here?"

"Yes."

"Why didn't they kill me?"

"I'm sure they would have done readily enough," the girl said, "but they had been given orders not to."

"By your father?"

"I imagined that obvious."

"Who got his from Luke Fletcher?" Trunch asked, his tones suggesting that that might not be quite so obvious — and that he did know more than she probably imagined.

Anger writhed in Janet Gibson's lips and flashed in her eyes. "Don't mention that man's name near me!" she hissed.

Trunch peered at her closely,

wondering. "That doesn't answer me."

The dark girl shrugged, a hardness present now that made her a woman indeed. "I am my father's daughter," she said. "When my mother died a few years ago, I took over the house — because it was my duty. I wash and sew and cook and clean, and I don't allow myself to think much beyond that. I fear a lot goes on around the ranch that I'd rather didn't go on, but — men are men and born to be as foolish as they like. Or so I've been brought up to believe. I'm careful to see nothing, hear nothing, and say even less. That way, I lead a quiet life."

"You've got your head screwed on right," Trunch acknowledged flatly, wincing as he felt at his own again. "So long as you don't go thinking the men in your life are good examples of the sex. Your papa was ever a dubious quantity, and the Adam I knew was pure poison. I wouldn't give the pair of them the time of day. But how'm

I to deny they've got me where they want me?"

The girl's right ear tilted abruptly, and she threw an anxious look across the bed towards the door of the room. "Did you hear anything?" she asked in a quick, low voice.

"No," he answered.

Her expression still unsure, Janet Gibson went on: "I'm surprised dad and Adam have left me alone with you this long. Keep your voice down. If you get too noisy and active, they'll come upstairs and bind you. I'm sure you don't want that."

"Damn right, I don't!" he agreed. "What's in store for me, Janet?"

"I don't think I'm supposed to say."

"You say," he wheedled. "I'm not going to tell on you."

"Well — " she began reluctantly.

At that moment the door burst open. Through it a giant figure ducked, a wicked expression on the ill-defined features of his porky face. He glared at the girl, then leered at the prisoner. "Get

121

out of here, Janet!" he commanded, growling ferociously when the female hesitated. "You heard me — and I heard you!"

Features set, Janet Gibson walked around the foot of the bed and made for the exit, eyes averting as she came level with the giant. Then he seized her by the left arm, jerked her onwards as if she were no more than a large doll, and aimed a boot at her receding posterior, kicking her hard enough to send her stumbling out into whatever space existed beyond the threshold of the room.

That was too much for Trunch. Hurt though he had felt up to now, he swung his legs off the bed and stood up on the floor to his left — scything a blow at the big man's midriff as he erected, and his fist buried itself wrist-deep in the mass of relaxed flesh and muscle that it encountered over the other's solar plexus. The giant hinged forward, and Trunch immediately straightened him with an uppercut. After that he hooked with his left, and banged over a similar right, the punches landing on either side of the big guy's jaw and shaking him down to his toes. "Lay off!" he spluttered.

The demand was like the proverbial red rag to a bull. Trunch promptly repeated the last treatment, following up now with a straight right to the mouth that threw the giant up against the wall and caused him to rebound in a fashion that set his knees buckling. Fully in vein by this time, Trunch gathered himself for the finisher, but he had still to trigger the ultimate blow, when an older man of about his own shape and make stepped into the room, pistol advanced, and pressed the muzzle of the weapon to Trunch's breastbone, saying: "Know any reason why I shouldn't blow the stuffing out of you, Ben Trunch?"

"Can't say as I do," the younger man responded grimly. "Would it make any difference to you anyhow? Life was always a trial with you Gibsons, and I don't suppose you've learned any better in the last fifteen years or so."

"You insulting young skunk!" Billy Gibson roared.

"You're a savage, and the father of a savage!" Trunch snarled back. "You'll get from me only the respect you deserve! I doubt that animal you call a son is even housetrained!"

"I'll kill you!" Billy Gibson screamed, almost beside himself as he danced on the spot.

"Then get on with it," Trunch gritted defiantly — "and answer to Luke Fletcher afterwards!"

"Oh, pa!" the slowly recovering giant exclaimed dazedly, blood leaking from either side of his split mouth and bruises rising all over the lower part of his face. "He done took me by surprise, pa! It was no fair fight!"

"Any man who kicks his sister deserves to be hit in the mouth!" Trunch spat. "That's a nice girl, and my only regret is that I didn't hit you hard enough to take the head clean off

124

your shoulders, Adam!"

"Now there you've got it!" Billy Gibson declared disgustedly. "You and Adam have always hated the sight of one another. This goes back to when you were kids. Ben, you're a blamed fool! You shouldn't have come home! If it was due to your father, you've wasted your effort. He's tight in his grave, and it's over and done with. God help us! You're the last of his blood, and there'll be dirt on top of you shortly!"

"Fate, Billy," Trunch said resignedly. "Just fate."

"Pa," Adam Gibson said, "I want you to call the men out and have the yard lit."

"What's that, noodle?" the rancher demanded sharply.

"I want you to have the yard lighted up — so's I can whale the tar out of Ben Trunch!"

"Do you?" Billy Gibson said nastily. "Then want will have to be your master, my man!"

"Please, pa!" the giant begged.

"Adam, you haven't the brains of a louse!" his father informed him, making a dismissive gesture. "He's already hided you so thoroughly I doubt if you're fit to crawl into bed. Do you want him to kill you? That's a tiger of a fighting man, and you're no better than a fat bear. The likes of you have never had a chance against the likes of him. But you're so young and inexperienced — and taken up with your own stupid size — that you think you can beat anybody. You know nothing — not a blind thing that counts!"

"Pa!"

"Don't keep paing me, Adam!" Billy Gibson snapped. "Take your unsightly ass off downstairs!"

"You're in one o' your consarned moods!" Adam declared, giving Trunch a terrible glance. "You ain't keeping your mind on the job. We've got to tie that sidewinder up. Can you see anybody coming here for him tonight?"

126

"Yes, I can," the rancher retorted. "If I'm any judge of Luke Fletcher, he'll want Ben Trunch in town this very night and placed safely under lock and key. Remember, it was getting on when I sent word to town that we'd got Trunch here. We'd had to make sure the fellow was going to live. You've got to give it time, Adam. Miles Grove is a fair distance away."

"What five miles?" the giant pooh-poohed. "Ain't nothing! Somebody ought to have got here long ago."

"Five miles across a dark land," Gibson reminded.

"What are you going to do with the varmint then?"

"Take him downstairs," Gibson said. "There's abundance in the kitchen. Feed him likely. Fletcher will want him kept in sound condition for the hanging. You know Luke! He can't bear to take the life of a man who's suffering. Says it's no more than putting the guy out of his misery."

"Son of a bitch!"

"At that," the rancher conceded, dislike revealing itself in both his voice and expression as he gazed downwards in an apparent attempt to see through the bedroom floor and into the lower part of the house, "we've little cause to love him."

"Aw, stop bemoanin' that sister of mine!" Adam snorted contemptuously. "She's just another girl who ain't no better than she should be."

"Faugh!" Gibson exclaimed, his mouth puckering in disgust. "Her cries for help had been heard all over town. Luke raped her!"

"The folk who found 'em together in Fletcher's stables didn't say so," Adam retorted. "There she was spread, her clothes all over the place, and Fletcher bouncing on top of her." He expressed his indifference in a gesture. "Women! It's what they're for, ain't it? Fletch don't pay us fair and square, that's what I've got against him!"

"We do come too cheap," Gibson admitted, "but you have to see all sides. We're only hosting cows on grass we don't need. There's no real danger to us; other men do the stealing. Don't dwell on it! You know that old saying, boy. He who sups with the devil must use a long spoon!"

"There's risk, pa."

"We're not innocent, but he does rule the roost."

"Through Ray Porlee."

"Who's denying it?" the rancher inquired acidly, everything about him hardening visibly again. "I'm not going up against Porlee — are you? You'd be some use! Go on downstairs, blast you! I told you just now! Don't you listen to anything, numskull?"

Adam Gibson swore to himself and slid Trunch another glance of the most terrible hatred. "I'll get you yet!" he hissed, spittle flying from between his tombstone teeth.

"Any time," Trunch answered blithely, licking a skinned knuckle.

"That's enough of that, Trunch!" Billy Gibson rapped, eye and gun firmly on the ex-sergeant as his son left the room. "Don't push me too hard, Ben! I'm a different kettle of fish from that boy of mine!"

Trunch gave the cattleman a cold smile and a nod of agreement.

"Downstairs," Gibson ordered. "Move out ahead of me — and don't give me cause to get worried!"

Trunch walked by the man. Gibson immediately closed up behind him, and he felt the muzzle of the rancher's gun press against his spine when they reached the door. He stepped out into a passage. This extended for several yards to his left but joined a lamplit landing only a short distance away to his right. A protective rail paralleled the left-hand side of the walk, and he followed this to the head of the stairs, where he turned onto the steps and pursued them downwards through a descent which brought him into the hall below.

He saw an open door in the wall opposite the bottom step, and glimpsed the comfortable furnishings in the drawing room beyond; but, as he made to go straight on and enter, he felt Billy Gibson's gun barrel chop lightly on the outside of his right shoulder and heard the cattleman tell him to turn left. This took him into the back of the hall and then the ranch kitchen, where he saw Janet Gibson considering a spillage stain on the cooking range and her brother Adam sprawled in a wooden armchair, legs apart and arms hanging loosely. The giant had a pout on his lips that made his piggy features more porcine than ever. "Do you have to bring him in here, pa?" he demanded. "He makes the place look untidy!"

Gibson ignored his son. "Go and sit at the table, Trunch," the rancher ordered.

Pulling out a straight-backed chair, Trunch obeyed, seating himself at the scrub-topped table which occupied the middle of the kitchen floor.

"Give him some grub, Janet," Gibson now commanded.

"If it's all the same to you, Billy," Trunch said as inoffensively as he could, "I won't eat anything. I came a rare old cropper this afternoon."

The rancher nodded, seeming perfectly reasonable about it. "If that's it, okay."

"That's it," Trunch assured him. "My stomach's all shook up."

"Won't you have a glass of milk, Ben?" the girl suggested, mildly solicitous.

"Thank you, no," Trunch responded. "I reckon even that's more than my frail digestion could manage at this minute."

"What a poor sap!" Adam jeered. "He ain't even a milksop!"

"Have a look in the glass, son!" his father advised contemptuously. "Must you keep it up?"

The big man fingered his bruised mouth. "I told you — I was took by surprise!"

"I heard you say."

"You ain't going to keep him sittin' there like that, are you?" Adam demanded aggrievedly. "The sight of his face is more than I can stand all night!"

"Where do you want to put him then?" Bill Gibson asked.

"The old pantry's good enough for him," Adam replied. "The window's only big enough to squeeze putty through, and the lock's solid iron."

"All right," the rancher said. "I don't see any objection to that. He has to go somewhere. Get up, you!"

Trunch got to his feet again, backing away from the table and returning his chair to its original unobtrusive position. Now he watched Adam rise from his armchair with a sudden alacrity and cross the room to a door at its further end. This he opened, revealing a darksome passage beyond which the light from the kitchen penetrated only dimly.

"Through there, Ben!" Billy Gibson snapped.

Trunch crossed the room. He passed Adam, who leered down cruelly at him, and entered the gloomy corridor, seeing a couple of doors on either hand. Following up closely behind the prisoner, Gibson senior opened the first door on the left, while Gibson junior came through also and struck a match; then, moving a little way beyond the other two men, he lighted a lamp hanging from the ceiling and brought a good glow right down the passage to the barred door at its further end.

"Get inside!" Gibson senior commanded, giving the captive a shove to start him into his prison.

Trunch stepped forward. He entered a little room that was perhaps eight feet long and no more than four across. Empty shelves banked on either side and across the back of the place, and the atmosphere was filled with a stony smell and the heat of the day. He turned slowly on his heel, absorbing the details without enthusiasm, and he was barely facing the threshold again when the door banged shut and he heard a key briefly squeak and grind in the lock.

Accepting the slight shock which the sound brought, Trunch held himself still and listened intently to whatever was happening at the other side of the door. He picked up the muttered word or two which passed between the father and son standing out there, then heard their footfalls move back into the kitchen and the connecting door shut with a loud click. After that there was almost total silence in the vicinity of the disused pantry.

Folding his arms, Trunch retreated until his back met the support of the shelves at the rear of the little room. There he leaned, feeling more dead than alive and frankly wondering what the devil next. He had sacrificed himself for Charlie Stokes and those other men from the brush, but he still didn't know whether his rather impromptu effort to buy them time had come off. It would be a definite consolation to know that those fellows had made it back to the safety of the thickets. Not that he had any great faith in them as a force for the future. They had their motive, and they didn't lack intelligence or ability, but they were without real driving force. A big purpose, especially when it involved life and limb, needed the ruthless mind of a hard man behind it, but he suspected that Charlie Stokes — the nominal leader of that outraged bunch — was more petulant than tough.

Trunch believed that Stokes and his friends lived too much in their imaginations and succeeded in achieving enough there to make them tentative in real life, and that could well have had a lot to do with how they had come to lose their all to Luke Fletcher in the first place. Luke was pure evil of the most calculating and determined kind and, while they knew it, they couldn't quite comprehend the conquering power of right. Underlying fear was their main weakness. To win, they would have to give battle with all their hearts, and realize that victory — when it did come — would only come by the breadth of a hair; because that was the nature of victory in all the big fights between good and bad men. Nothing less than total commitment would do. He never fought with less, but those guys really didn't know what it was. They needed him all right. But it looked as if their need was going to be denied. If indeed they had survived that afternoon.

About half an hour went by. Trunch breathed audibly in the warm density of the abandoned larder's air. His concentration balanced on a razor's edge. Then a cautious sound reached him. He knew that the connecting door had been opened again, and that somebody was entering the passage outside from the kitchen. He waited tensely, quite sure that whoever it was had business with him — of a private kind — and he wondered whether it could be Janet Gibson out there. With all her pretence of being just another weak and compliant female, he had sensed steel in her nature, and he was convinced that she did not approve of how the men in her family were treating him. He was certain, too, that she could have no wish to further Luke Fletcher's cause, since nothing bred hatred of a man in the female like being raped by him. And Trunch did not doubt that that was what had happened to her — even though it could have appeared otherwise to witnesses. For he had always believed it wiser for a woman to submit to a violator than to risk her life by putting up an impossible fight. Thus, it was just possible that Janet was going to —

The key twisted abruptly in the lock, and the pantry door opened likewise. Trunch saw at once that it was not the girl who stood outside in the light from the hanging-lamp but her brother Adam. Swallowing his disappointment, Trunch prepared himself for what he knew must come.

6

BRACED up, Trunch watched the big man take a stride into the bare pantry. He advanced to meet the other by half a pace. They stood face to face, an electric air between them. "Pa gone to bed?" Trunch inquired mockingly.

"No business of yours!" Adam Gibson snarled, his features livid.

"You've worked yourself into a fine old state, haven't you?" Trunch observed, as sardonic as he was contemptuous. "You great lout, you haven't the self-control of a baby! You'll never grow up, Adam! It takes a man to learn from a thrashing!"

"It was no fair fight," the giant rasped.

"It wasn't a fight at all," Trunch said. "I let into you, and that's the fact of it."

"Trunch, I could beat you any day of the week!"

"Who gives a damn?"

"You do."

A chuckle, small and brittle, left Trunch's lips. "Only so far as it hurts."

"I owe you for that day in the brush!" the big man declared. "I ain't never lived it down, and I'm going to cripple you for that, Trunch!"

Trunch nerved himself anew; for he realized that, even though his enemy was almost beside himself, Adam meant exactly what he said. A shudder passed through the lighter man, and with it came visions of lying on an invalid bed for the rest of his days, with others reluctantly taking care of him in what could only be the most humiliating of circumstances. He felt that he would rather die here and now than end his days broken in limb and spirit; but he also determined there and then that Adam would have to pay a big price for any final victory over him. Yet whatever he did would have to be done quickly, for he still felt very weak and ill from yesterday's fall and realized that his power to absorb new punishment was very limited. "Adam," he said persuasively, wondering if even now the struggle could be avoided, "this is all foolish pride. Your father is going to bite bits out of you for it. It isn't worth it."

"I don't care what," the fleshy Gibson almost choked, "but I'm going to lam you until you ain't got one unbroken bone left!"

Adam attacked as the last word left his lips. His movement had all the suddenness of so much that had gone before. But Trunch had been waiting for it and was in no degree surprised. Diving headlong, he passed between the straight punches which the restricting width of the larder forced his attacker to throw at him — since he was determined not to take any blows before he had to — and the sheer desperation of his movement carried him through. He cannoned off Adam — who was virtually defenceless in that moment, with arms extended — then, seizing the other's body, spun around it and ended at his enemy's back, left arm thrust across the giant's throat and anchored by the pressure of its fist under his own right armpit. With this much done, he immediately slapped his free palm against the side of Adam's chin and forced it round to the left, the whole creating a hold that was a potential neck-breaker.

After that it was almost entirely down to strength and willpower. Trunch threw everything he had into maintaining his grip, while the ponderous Gibson threshed this way and that, seeking to throw him off, but the big man lacked both the knowledge and the wrestling skill to break the hold. Adam went from absolute confidence to something like panic as he discovered that raw power was not the answer to his troubles, and now he too flung his all into the struggle, finally drawing on his imagination to crush and pump his adversary among the shelves along the walls as he had not done to begin with; but nothing availed, and the pressure on his neck only increased as he gradually exhausted himself and Trunch was able to find a corner and fix himself into it, thus securing his stance and enabling him to hold the bigger man to the same spot.

All at once Adam let out a beaten gasp. His upper body relaxed involuntarily and his knees gave a trifle. Now Trunch sent in still more strength behind his right hand, and he sensed that the threat to Adam's spine was becoming acute. A very little extra pressure would snap the big man's neck like a carrot. Sobs of agony were choking their way through Adam's distorted lips — yet the man still offered no plea for mercy. "Do you want to die?" Trunch breathed. "Promise to behave — or, so help me, I'll finish you off!"

Somehow Adam came together with a jolt and began to resist again, and Trunch feared that he would have to carry out his threat — for the big man was either much braver or more foolish than he had imagined — but just then a figure appeared in the doorway of the disused pantry and Trunch saw that it was Billy Gibson, Adam's father, gun in hand. "Let him go, Trunch," the older man warned — "or I'll blow a hole in you!"

Making himself small, Trunch stood virtually hidden by the towering Adam's mass and he decided quite cold-bloodedly to take everything here to the limit if he must. "No, Billy!" he countered. "You've got it wrong. Your son and heir is only an inch from death. Toss your gun over to me — or, by all that we hold sacred, I'll break Adam's neck!" He put out the rest of his strength, holding back on only the final twist, and a despairing gurgle issued from the giant's gullet. "Well?"

"Don't do it!" Billy Gibson cried aghast, capitulating after only an instant's hesitation, and he sent his revolver flying into the corner where his son's life was being so imminently threatened.

Hearing the gun clatter down on the stone floor, Trunch once again put out his strength and propelled Adam towards the man standing on the threshold of the little room. Adam went blundering and reeling towards his father, and had no control over himself as his bulk collided with Billy's much lighter frame. Carried by his impetus, the two men staggered out into the corridor at Gibson senior's back and collapsed in a heap.

Trunch snatched up the gun from the floor. Holding it before him, he plunged out into the passage — intending to make his escape from the house through the kitchen — but he had barely emerged from the pantry door, with eyes down to make sure that he avoided the two men writhing there, when a shot cracked out and a bullet literally plucked the pistol from his outstretched hand.

"Hold it, Trunch!" a not unfamiliar

voice warned; and, shocked by both the explosion and what the bullet had done, Trunch stopped in his tracks and looked quickly to the right, where he saw the huge figure of Sheriff Carl Ives standing in the doorway that connected the passage with the kitchen. The lawman held a smoking Colt in his right fist and had already cocked it again. "Out here!"

Feeling somewhat crushed by this latest example of a supreme effort in vain — but recognising that there was nothing else for it — Trunch lifted his hands and walked towards the sheriff, who backed off into the kitchen and halted between the table and the cooking range, thus ensuring that a safe gap remained between him and the ex-sergeant as he gestured for Trunch to stop a single pace inside the room. "It seems I got here in the nick of time," he said triumphantly. "None of this is going to help you a scrap, Ben."

"Carl," Trunch cautioned, "when

last comes to last, you're elected law. You dare not stand by openly and permit a lynching. I know you're on the take from Luke Fletcher — that much was plain to me this morning — but you can only get away with so much and keep your job. Let the man in the street once suspect you're rotten all through — and you're finished!"

"What the hell are you gabbing about?" Ives scorned, his crude, brick-red features alight with indignation. "I'm taking you in for trial. You're a triple murderer! Can you deny that you shot three men to death in the Big T ranch yard this morning?"

"Yes, I shot three men there," Trunch admitted. "It was a gunfight; I shot only in self-defence. Those guys had orders from Luke Fletcher to kill me. If you want to hold somebody for murder, Sheriff, you hold Luke Fletcher. He gunned down Ernie Wheeler before my eyes!"

"Heard about it."

"You're in trouble too, Carl, and this

is your best way out of it."

"I'm in no trouble!" Ives scorned.
"That's you speaking! The undertaker's
men have already stated that Luke
had to shoot. Ernie had just tossed
you a gun, and was trying to draw
another one."

"That's a wicked lie!"

"Tell that to the witnesses."

"Bought men!"

"You'll have to prove that in court,"
Ives said. "Those bearers are respected
townsmen. Can you prove it? Have you
any witnesses of your own?"

"This is a frame up!" Trunch
seethed.

"Innocent men don't run away from
the scene of the crime," Ives reminded.
"It's *all* against you."

"No," Trunch groped. "There's a
cow cache on the Gibson ranch. It's
over at Wolf Bottoms. An attempt
was made to murder me and others
there. It all fits in with Fletcher's dirty
doings. I'm sure there are plenty of folk
around here who're bright enough to

know there's a crafty land-grab afoot and that rustling is rife. If all that's properly investigated — and brought out in court — Fletcher's going to have to do some fast talking. Much of what's against *him* is self-evident."

"Spare me!" Ives pleaded. "Luke Fletcher has come by his gains through honest business moves. He's nothing to fear. It's always been a hard world for the loser. And if you're pinning any hopes on those malcontents hiding out in the brush, forget 'em! We've known about them and their grievances for weeks. If they get dangerous, we'll soon flush the varmints out; but they haven't been dangerous — in fact they haven't been anything at all up to now — and that's why they're still riding around free. Give it a while, Ben, and they'll just fade away. Be sure of that — after you've been hanged!"

Trunch tried to go on with it, but he no longer had any real counter arguments or the words to express them. He felt utterly hemmed in. The web of evil that contained him appeared to have no weaknesses among its threads. It was the devil's work indeed. Yet he had been taught that the devil's work was never perfect. The Lord of Misrule spun a false yarn. There had to be a flaw somewhere in this texture of lies. But he couldn't spot it — and absolute desperation surged in him again.

His thoughts simply flew. He considered a last bid to escape. But some stiffening of his spirit must have been detectable to the men behind him, for he heard a revolver back there in the passage click on cock and knew that the instant he hurled himself into action a bullet from Billy Gibson would strike him down. All was totally against him, and his face must have given some recognition of this too, for Carl Ives tipped back his head and vented a sneering laugh. "Out there in the yard!" he called. "D'you hear me, Hobbs? Bring the shackles inside!"

The back door was ajar. Movements — which included the faintly musical rattling of chains — were audible outside. Then the door turned inwards and a stocky man of medium height and dour features entered, the lamplight glinting on both the deputy's star pinned to the front of his waistcoat and the new steel chains and cuffs which he held before him. "Carl?" he asked meekly.

"Chain Ben Trunch up, Hobbs!" the sheriff ordered. "Make a job of it now — or you'll hear all about it from me when we get back to the office!"

"Yes, sir," Hobbs said, his smirking subservience a little sickening.

"Making a big thing of it, aren't you, Carl?" Trunch taunted, determined that he would show no trace of fear in whatever lay before him.

"Paying due respect," Ives jeered in return. "You're as slippery as any rattlesnake, and I'm going to make good and sure you don't dodge the gallows."

"That's a hanging I'll be at!" Adam Gibson promised, his voice thick and shaky as he edged back into the room from the prisoner's rear. "I want to get real close to the drop, Carl, and hear the crack when his neck goes!"

"He spared you, Adam," the big man's father reminded stonily. "But I guess that counts for nothing."

"Not a thing, Billy," the sheriff agreed. "There's no way you can excuse murder. Get the trial over, and we'll have him dead and buried in twenty-four hours."

Now there was a chilling thought. Standing motionless, Trunch did his best to assimilate it, but he couldn't quite conceal the shudder that passed through his limbs from the man who was chaining his upper body, and the servile Hobbs grinned at the sheriff and winked. "These here are the same chains you'll be wearing on the drop!" he advised. "With a shake and rattle, you'll drop ass-first onto the devil's pitchfork!"

"Get on with it," Ives said shortly.

Face lengthening, Hobbs gave all

his attention to his work, and a few moments later he said: "That'll hold him, Sheriff. His legs I'll fix when he's got on his horse."

Ives nodded. "Into the yard, Trunch!"

Hands manacled before him, Trunch started rounding the kitchen table and heading for the back door, the steel links that trailed about his nether limbs jingling as he walked. He sensed a small movement to his right, and darted a glance towards it, seeing Janet Gibson framed in the doorway which gave access to the hall. The dark girl's face was expressionless. She seemed barely aware of what was taking place, and somehow it angered and hurt him that she should appear so detached and uncaring. Pointing his chin at her, he said: "You can't sit on the fence, girl. When they go, they'll take you down with them."

"Enough of your lip, Ben!" Ives snapped.

Hobbs emphasized the point with a well-placed kick.

Glancing over his shoulder, Trunch let the deputy see how he felt about that abuse with a flinty eye which expressed cold rage. Hobbs paled a little, but there could be no more to it than that, and the prisoner passed out of the house and into the relative darkness of a ranch yard that was unevenly pricked out by hanging lanterns. Here he dimly perceived that several other horsemen were present, and he acknowledged inwardly that Carl Ives was indeed showing him 'due respect', but he imagined that the sheriff had in fact considered the possibility of a nocturnal rescue from the brush and simply ensured that whatever happened on his round trip to the Broken G, the gunpower would favour him.

The deputy guided the captive to a horse, and Trunch realized from the animal's size and shape that it was Sheila Wilson's strawberry mare. He was glad that the brute had not been injured by the heavy collision in which it had been involved that afternoon and, catching at the front of the saddle with his cuffed hands, he speared the nearside stirrup and heaved himself astride the docile horse, sitting erect while Hobbs locked the previously dragging lengths of chain under the mount's barrel and then put the reins in his hands.

"That'll do, Fred," Sheriff Ives announced, mounting up himself and watching Hobbs follow his example. "All right, men, close up around the prisoner and let's get him back to town. The sooner the job's done, the sooner you all get to bed!"

With Trunch totally hemmed in, the party moved off, soon picking up an ill-defined path which headed eastwards — by a glance at the North Star — and the ride went forward without check of any kind. Prisoner and escort steadily crossed the grassy miles which rolled blackly against the lower stars and, still without any occurrence to disturb the tenor of the night, entered

Miles Grove about three-quarters of an hour later. The time was now well advanced — around midnight, Trunch judged — but there was still a certain amount of activity on the main street and plenty of noise coming from the saloons. Knowing his arrival in town to be of the greatest importance to Luke Fletcher, Trunch expected the saloonkeeper to be around to see him locked up, but there was no sign of the man when the law party halted outside the sheriff's office, and this remained how it was when the prisoner was taken indoors, unchained, searched, put through a mock interrogation, and locked up in the jailhouse. Indeed it was almost with a sense of neglect that Trunch stretched out on the cot in his cell and lay staring into the shadows of the grim and poorly lighted building that enclosed him. Yet, if Luke Fletcher were absent now, he felt pretty sure that he would be seeing far more than enough of the man in the near future. Anyhow, the scene matched his plight and mood — and he could have suffered dreadfully — but he was also tired out, and it was not long before fatigue overcame misery and he went to sleep.

It was with a sickening start that he awoke again. He was still lying on his back, but found himself staring out into the daylight which now filled the passage beyond the bars of his cage. The night could have passed at the stroke of a finger. He felt rested, yes, but his state of fear had not diminished and every aspect of the case against him rose up in naked detail to test his courage. If the evidence involved went unchallenged by the truth itself, he'd hang all right. The witnesses might be false ones, but he'd shot those three men in front of them okay, and his flight from the Tumbleweed saloon and the Rakes business could be made to look black indeed. Doubtless he was taking a very depressed view of things but, in the main, he was seeing clearly enough.

For his own peace of mind, Trunch forced his attention further afield. He heard snatches of muttered talk from the office which adjoined the jailhouse. Concentrating hard, he tried to latch on to the sense of what was being said, but made out nothing of any real account, and was still straining his ears, when a tired-looking Carl Ives entered the cell block in an almost silent fashion and stopped outside his door, peering in at him through the bars. "Morning, Ben," he said. "You look about as bad as I feel."

"God help us then!" Trunch yawned.

"Aren't you the lucky one!"

"Oh, yeah!" Trunch returned. "Change places?"

Ives smiled faintly. "You can sleep all day if you want to. And will, if you've got any sense. I've lawyers arguing over you already — but I reckon it'll be tomorrow before they come in to meet you and start preparing their cases."

"Farce. That's what they call it, don't they?"

"No. Fair trial."

"Do you really figure you can get away with this, Carl?"

"More of that persuasion, eh?" Ives observed sarcastically. "You're getting to be a bore, Ben. What do you want for breakfast?"

"Whatever you're prepared to give me."

"Now there's sense."

Trunch bared his teeth. "Do you expect me to sit back and just wait for it to happen?"

"Why not?" Ives asked brazenly. "That's how it's going to be."

"Mister, this is just too cut-and-dried!" Trunch responded, suddenly confident about what he said. "It's going to catch up with you!"

"When you're under the ground?" the sheriff inquired, his chuckle dry and taunting.

"There's a God up there somewhere!"

"Don't pile it on!" Ives rasped disdainfully. "Time enough to seek consolation of the church, boy, the hour before you hang. This holy stuff don't suit your cut!" He pulled a wry jib. "Aw, you make me sick! Where's the iron in you? You'll get a plate of scrambled egg — and like it!"

"Sure," Trunch said, closing his eyes and lying back on the bag of wool that served as a pillow. "Didn't I say?"

The sheriff turned away from the bars of the cage. Muttering to himself, he walked back into his office, haw-hawing in further disdain of religious consolation and cowardice as he rejoined whoever it was that was sharing duty with him just then. After that he kicked the connecting door shut, and the voices in the office were once more reduced to the muttering which had been audible to the captive before.

Trunch burned briefly, then dismissed his exchange with Ives as of no account. He felt his imprisonment more with every minute that went by — and the nerve-inflaming frustration of it — but he had enough experience to know that what he was going through could play havoc with the emotions and end in panic. Nothing made a worse spectacle of a man than panic, or more surely confirmed his gutlessness — and that was not to mention what it did to his energies and reasoning powers — so Trunch willed himself into a doze and completely calmed down, determined to keep an even mind and indicate his innocence whenever he could. Most lawyers were honest men, and he might be able to impress his essential honesty on those with whom he had to deal. For it was a fact that truth had a ring of its own, and he was going to need friends in court. Yet, through it all, there was something nightmarish and overstressed about what was happening to him — something that his personal integrity wanted to laugh at or ignore — but the unreal was real, and this life, so strong in him, was as deeply threatened as the thickening shadow of the nightmare suggested.

Presently Trunch's breakfast was brought through to his cell. It was in the hands of a dark, taciturn deputy whom the captive had never met before. The other eyed him sternly, while passing in his tray through the slot forged for such purposes in the bars of the door, and issued a brief warning that Sheriff Ives and Fred Hobbs, the second deputy, had just gone off duty, leaving him in charge. He said that his name was Harry Clay, and he would take no old buck, so the prisoner had better keep a civil tongue in his head and behave himself — or else!

Shrugging, Trunch didn't bother to inquire into the 'or else' but spooned down his promised scrambled egg and drank the mug of heavily sweetened coffee that came with it. That done, he paced his cell for a few minutes, aiding appetite, then went back to his cot and the renewed contemplation of both the ceiling and his plight. He felt the better for the food, since he had been badly underfed during the last two days, and it occurred to him that this might account for some part of his low spirits.

As the morning wore on, his fear and tedium mingled and became one. He kept quiet, and was left entirely to himself. A cooked meal was carried in to him during the early part of the afternoon, and he ate again, getting another lift from the grub. After that, restored in full to his lonely silence, he drifted off into a doze that lasted for the next hour or two and only ended when he heard voices and footfalls approaching the cell block from the office. Sitting up on his cot, Trunch turned his feet to the floor and looked out through the bars of his cage. He watched three people walk up to his cell and stop outside. They were Harry Clay, the deputy, Sheila Wilson — her face carefully veiled by a corner of her Spanish shawl — and a big, lean figure clad in the habit of a Jesuit priest. "Hi, hoss thief!" the woman greeted, her jeer almost lost in the coldness of her voice. "The word's out you're in need

163

of spiritual consolation. I've brought you some."

Rising, Trunch considered the trio with a doubtful eye. He wasn't sure he needed any of this.

7

TRUNCH felt his face begin hardening, and he was on the verge of telling Sheila Wilson and the priest to go back whence they'd come, when the woman shifted the veiling corner of her shawl for a moment and revealed split lips, a somewhat flattened nose, a contused left eyebrow, and a bruising of the rest of the face which had so altered her normal beauty that she looked like an ugly old hag. Obviously she had received a terrible beating — and Trunch was pretty certain that it had been Luke Fletcher's work — yet it wasn't so much the revelation of the facial damage that caught his attention as the swift passing glint of cautionary light in the woman's good right eye. In that instant Trunch sensed there could be more to this visit than Sheila's wish to mock him, and he caught at his tongue, letting an expression of amused indifference come to his face. "You're welcome," he drawled. "I reckon this is a poor place to welcome guests — but that's how it is."

"What's wrong with the place?" Deputy Sheriff Clay inquired aggressively, rattling his keys. "It's clean, the bed is more comfortable than a killer like you deserves, and the grub that comes in to you from Filby's restaurant is better than I get!"

"Sure, sure," Trunch soothed. "Take it easy, Harry! Ever hear a prisoner praise his prison?"

"Less of the Harry!" Clay warned, not particularly mollified. "I'm going to unlock the door and let the father and Miss Wilson join you inside. You mind your manners now! I'll be standing out here, taking in all that's said, and woe betide you, Trunch, the first thing you say or do that ain't fitting. You got me?"

"Sure, sure," the captive soothed

again. "Would I want to rub you up the wrong way, Harry?"

"I told you about that, Trunch!"

"I can't help having a friendly nature — "

"Don't you dare!"

Trunch clasped his hands before him and meekly lowered his eyes.

Scowling, Clay unlocked the door of the cell and pushed it inwards, drawing his revolver and holding it cocked as Sheila Wilson and the Jesuit priest entered. "Ah, my son!" the holy man said, his Spanish accent just noticeable. "This is a sorry hour for you! You appear to have done great wrong before God and man, and I fear your days upon this earth are growing few. But be of good cheer! Who but God knows the final purpose of what we do? Life is a journey of the spirit, and the body a mere vehicle — an encumbrance even! Its death means nothing, and you may be sure that you will pass into realms — "

"Thanks," Trunch interrupted, chilled

by this blithe promise of a better life beyond the grave. "Let's get through the trial first."

"You don't expect to beat the charges, Ben?" Sheila Wilson protested. "Courts hang murderers and horse thieves in this part of Texas!"

"I'll lay you got your nag back," Trunch retorted. "And a real nice horse it is too."

"It was still stolen."

"If you say so, lady!" Trunch snorted.

The lawman banged the cage door shut, enjoining more caution. "Behave, Trunch — behave!"

The priest smiled across his shoulder, silently begging the deputy sheriff to take no offence. "We mean you only well, my son," he then said to the prisoner in a reassuring voice. "Please be seated."

"I'll let the lady sit down," Trunch responded, peering deeply into the Jesuit's lined and dubiously ascetic face, and wondering what make of saint they had here — for there was no aura of holiness surrounding his berobed visitor — but he realized that you could not always judge a man by his presence and knew that many who wore the monkish habit were forced by circumstances to be rather worldly men. They had to survive the times. "Have a seat, Sheila. The bed is the only one I have to offer."

"Quit apologising, Ben," the woman said, walking over to the cell cot and sitting down on its foot. "I've sat on a man's bed before today."

"No treat there," Trunch said dryly. "Carl Ives has got something to answer for. I didn't know he'd got such a big mouth — or you were such a fool."

"You've lived a bad life, Ben," Sheila Wilson accused.

"I wouldn't rate it perfect myself," Trunch admitted. "But others have lived a heck of a lot worse."

"Does that absolve you?"

"No, but — "

"I want you to leave this world

properly shriven," the woman said. "Let Deputy Sheriff Harry Clay bear witness to my words."

"I heard you, Miss Wilson," the deputy growled, looking as mystified as the prisoner and even more unimpressed. "I'd say it's a pure waste of time. From what I've heard, there's no way he's gettin' into heaven. St Peter will pick him up by the scruff of his neck and drop him back to the foot of the gallows."

"No sinner who repents is ever excluded from the Divine Grace," the Jesuit chided. "Though your sins be as scarlet, yet shall they be washed white as snow. Oh, ye of little faith!"

"It's the most I can do for you, Ben," Sheila Wilson said seriously. "This is the act of a friend. All you have to do is listen."

There had been a hope of rescue in Trunch after picking up that swift glint in Sheila Wilson's eye; but now he was ninety-nine percent certain that he had misread the woman's glance. She had not been hinting at derring-do, but had simply feared that he was about to behave in a manner that would get her and the priest returned to the street. There had been no more to her apparently covert reaction than that. It was a further disappointment, and Trunch felt correspondingly deflated, but he reckoned he owed Sheila Wilson what she asked — regardless of her motives. "So what's the father's name then?" he asked.

"I am Frey Miguel Angelo," the priest said. "I am an itinerant of the House of the Society of Jesus in Mexico City."

"Nice ring to it, Father," Trunch observed. "Means Michael the Angel, doesn't it?"

"It is merely the name by which I am known in this world," the priest responded with dignity. "This woman has a care for your soul, my son. I am here to ensure that you fall into the arms of Our Saviour and not those of the Beast on your fatal day." He drew himself up. "This ministry depends upon your will. If you are set upon an eternity of hellfire, we will depart and trouble you no more."

"I'll listen, Father," Trunch said. "It can't hurt even an innocent man to get some Bible-teaching, I guess."

"Good for you, Ben," Sheila Wilson approved, rising. "My part's done. I'll leave you in the safe hands of Father Miguel."

"Well, okay," Trunch said with surprise, as he watched her walk to the cell door. "Didn't quite figure on you pulling out. Not much company in that."

"My part is done," she repeated.

He twitched a shoulder, a trifle miffed. "See you at the hanging," he said flippantly, regretting the words as soon as they were out; but the woman ignored them and quickly departed from the jailhouse, her shawl now concealing the whole of her ruined face.

"With the lady gone," Harry Clay

reflected, shooting the lock of the open cell door to make his point, "I reckon I can lock you two in. All right, Father?"

The priest nodded. "You must do your duty as you see fit, my son."

"Okay, Father," the deputy sheriff said, securing the cage and sauntering towards the office. "Just lift your voice when you're ready to leave. I'll be out at the desk."

"I will call you when I have finished," the Jesuit responded. "Peace be with you."

Alone with the priest, Trunch wondered what the deuce he had let himself in for — especially when he was asked to kneel on the stone floor and Father Miguel prayed over him for a minute or two — but, beyond that point, he was bewildered when the other dropped the ceremony and formalism of his office and started talking in a conversational manner about everyday things. It even seemed to Trunch at one moment that he could smell tobacco and something stronger than sacrificial wine on the holy man's breath. In fact it wasn't until a quarter of an hour later, when Father Miguel said that he must be leaving now, that he moved back from the secular to the sacred again and blessed the prisoner in the name of the Father, Son, and Holy Ghost, called the deputy back to the cell door, and then departed from the jailhouse with the promise that he would return on the morrow and bring further religious consolation. It was all rather sensitive and impressive, yet left the captive feeling that the visit had been somehow less than priestly and hardly what it had purported to be in any way at all.

Trunch spent the next hour or so pondering the matter. He wavered once more between an unsteady hope and a patchy despair. While he was sure that there was more to Father Miguel Angelo than met the eye, he was far from certain as to what it might be. Sheila Wilson had always been a most unpredictable woman and might be up to almost anything — or even pretending that she was — for her own amusement and his further discomfiture. Though he couldn't really believe the latter, for Sheila had never been a malicious woman and had no cause to pay him back for anything. Thus a mystery of sorts had manifested and could not be resolved; and the day finally became night and Trunch slept again — to awaken the next morning in a state of perplexity similar to that in which he had fallen asleep the night before.

His second day behind bars gave him still more to think about. He received visits from the legal gentry of the town and was closely questioned about all his recent journeys and actions. If untrained in legal matters, he soon perceived the shape of the case being built against him out of the lies that fitted the circumstantial evidence available, and he became increasingly convinced that even his defenders were no friends of his and that he was certainly going to hang for murder if this business went to the limit. He might protest that he had done no wrong at any juncture, and only defended himself when forced; but, while the undertaker's men went on swearing to the contrary, there was no hope of what had occurred in the Big T ranch yard being examined in its true light. All that had concerned the cheating Matt Rakes and Jack Trunch's suicide was no less artfully misrepresented and made to fit the rest of the damning picture. Indeed, even knowing the wickedness of his fellow men, he still found it hard to credit that such unscrupulous behaviour was going on around him, and there remained moments when he could not believe that any of it was actually happening.

It was into the evening before Father Miguel kept his promise and reappeared. He was let into Trunch's cell — by a grinning Sheriff Ives on this occasion — and prisoner and priest were again locked in and left together. The Jesuit went for a second time through the somewhat ambiguous performance which had marked his visit of the previous day, and he also departed again in much the same manner, promising a further visit around the same hour on the morrow, and Trunch was once more left to ponder the undercurrents and listen to an instinct which warned him to question nothing aloud and simply allow silence to seal the illusion of a zealous priest who was pressing salvation on a criminal who was surely bound for hellfire if he didn't repent.

Father Miguel's visits repeated through the next week. They became a habit which everybody in the sheriff's office began to accept as a matter of course. The atmosphere about the priest's meetings with the captive grew more and more relaxed, and Trunch was content to let the holy man drone on about anything at all — still clinging to the shaky belief that patience would at last reveal some deeper purpose to what was now clearly a religious charade — and it was with the date of the trial fixed and word out that the gallows were already being tested, that Father Miguel appeared in the jailhouse rather later than usual and offered the captive his latest 'instruction' in the dusk of the day.

Trunch went through another half an hour of prayer and small talk, and then Father Miguel called the man on duty — Deputy Sheriff Fred Hobbs in this case — to let him out of the prisoner's cell again. Hobbs appeared and the cage was unlocked in the normal fashion, the deputy rather carelessly turning his back as he pushed the door open, and it was in that moment that the revelation came; for Father Miguel, his hands hidden in the sleeves of his habit, stepped up behind the lawman and, a revolver appearing in the hand which slid from his left sleeve, threw up the steel barrel of the weapon and knocked Hobbs on the head. The deputy emitted a gasping grunt and started to collapse, and the priest caught him under the armpits and quickly lowered him against the bars which made up the wall of the cage on his right. Hobbs, quite unconscious now, sat there with his arms limp and his chin sagging upon his chest.

Turning now, the Jesuit put the revolver into Trunch's hand. Then he swung back on the senseless deputy and took the lawman's keys from the lock. After that, beckoning for the prisoner to follow him, he stepped out of the cell and went to the back door of the jailhouse where, swiftly going through the keys on the ring, he found the one that fitted the lock and opened the rear entrance onto the yard beyond. "I have a horse waiting," the priest whispered, looking narrowly back along the passage which led to the office, a raised finger enjoining strict quiet to ensure that no suspicious sound carried through to anybody who might be present there.

"Right!" Trunch breathed, amazed at what had taken place and that all had gone so smoothly thus far. "Show me to the critter!"

"Not for you," Father Miguel murmured, shaking his head. "You are needed here in town. My departure on horseback will be heard — and I shall be pursued — but nobody is going to catch me. Go quickly into the passage on the left side of this building. You will be met there. Goodbye, Trunch, and *buena suerte!*"

Trunch saluted with the muzzle of the gun that he was holding in his right hand. Then he catfooted swiftly to his left. He couldn't make any sense of what was happening now, but he had to accept that all this had been thought out well ahead of this moment and simply persist in the order that he had been given; so he turned into the head of the alley which the priest had indicated and peered down it towards the main street, immediately glimpsing a figure in the gloom before him.

Instinctively, he raised his weapon and thumbed back its hammer, advancing the muzzle threateningly; but a husky female voice promptly whispered: "No, Ben!"

"Sheila?"

"This way!"

He followed her down the length of the alley, and they paused at the edge of the main street. Turning their heads to left and right, they peered into the pools of lamp-starred night on either side of them and listened to the noises of the town — which included the stirring of horses at the hitching rails, the upraised voices of revellers amidst the tinny music of the saloons, somebody washing tin utensils under a pump, and a nearby dog dragging its chain — but there seemed to be no watcher in the vicinity to deter their further progress, and the woman put out a hand and drew Trunch across the street into the shadows of the sidewalk opposite. "All right, Ben?" she queried, when he stubbed a toe among the slats.

"Okay," he responded thickly, drawing a deep breath.

She plucked at his shirt again. They entered a second alley. This bore them through to the lots on the northern side of town. Here Sheila Wilson made a right turn. Her hems sweeping the dusty underfoot, she fled like a pale ghost down the backs of the dwellings adjacent. Trunch pursued her at a similar flat out pace and, knowing the littered nature of the ground which they were covering, was amazed that neither tripped and fell in the process. He could hardly credit it when they arrived without mishap at the rear of a private house towards the eastern end of the main street and the woman brought them to a stop.

Crouched to recover his breath again, Trunch made out the uprights and slanting roof of an awning on their right. Then he heard a door open at the back of the shelter, slivers of light tracing the movement, and he also glimpsed the dull glow of a lamp behind the thick and fully drawn curtains at a nearby window in the rear wall of the dwelling. "Sheila?" the voice of a second female asked tensely.

"Me," Sheila Wilson agreed breathlessly. "I've got him with me. It worked like a charm. Don't put the wood in the hole, honey! The sooner we're inside the better."

The woman just visible in the doorway opposite stepped aside. Sheila Wilson almost literally sprang past her, and Trunch leapt into the house also. Both he and his guide pulled up a yard or two down a passage which obviously connected the back of the house with the lighted hall beyond that ran along to the front entrance. Then, as they turned and stood watching, the woman at the back door closed up in their wake and walked quickly across the passage into the kitchen adjacent. Sheila Wilson entered at the other woman's heels, and Trunch pursued as a close third, seeing at once that the second female was the black-haired Janet Gibson from the Broken G. "What the heck are you doing here?" he gasped. "I didn't know you and Sheila were pals!"

"There's plenty you don't know, son," Sheila Wilson informed him. "The world doesn't need your permission to keep turning. We figured the best way to keep you out from beneath our feet would be to leave you in jail for a spell!"

"What's up with you women these days?" Trunch demanded hotly. "Who the devil was that priest you had keep visiting me?"

"His name is Luis Allende," Sheila answered chidingly. "And you might speak of the man with more respect. He's out riding his butt off for you right now!"

"Luis Allende?" Trunch puzzled his brains for a moment or two. "That wouldn't be the Mexican bandit of the name, would it?"

"The very same, Ben. Luis is an old friend of mine."

"One of the many, Sheila?"

"You care?"

"No. Just asking."

"Why bother?" Sheila Wilson taunted. "See why we had to keep you out of the picture?"

"I doubt it was quite that," Trunch growled. "Anyhow, that ruse of yours to get me out of jail was smart enough. It had those guys over in the law office completely fooled."

"It worked well enough."

"Must have cost you a packet."

"Favours of the kind don't come cheap," Sheila admitted. "But you can only measure the cost by what it buys."

"Now that's a fact!" Trunch conceded. "You're after Luke Fletcher's head on a plate."

"He's gone too far," Sheila said seriously. "He's got to be stopped. It ought to have happened before people began to die."

"I think my dad and I brought it to a head."

The older woman jerked her chin at

the silent Janet Gibson. "She saw it so. And, yes — I feel the same. Even though you're pretty much a worthless lump and your late pa was wedded to folly!"

Trunch winced inwardly, but smiled it off. "I'm going to pay Luke Fletcher for what he did to your face — and that's a solemn promise."

"Should you find yourself that close," Sheila Wilson said stonily, "kill him. Never trade blows with a rattler. Its bite is deadly poison!"

"I'll remember your words," Trunch assured her. "So what's the rest of this master plan?"

"It's not quite that," Janet Gibson now interrupted. "We're going to work the only way I can see how."

"You?"

"She's got more savvy than the pair of us put together, Ben," Sheila Wilson informed him. "I'm just a crafty old drab, and you'd lead us up a box canyon."

"I always did prefer folk who speak

their minds," Trunch said wryly, as he looked at Janet Gibson with an inquiring eye.

"I'm not especially bright, Ben," the younger woman said. "I'm only a girl trying to save the men of her family from themselves. Though, goodness knows, I'm not sure they're worth saving!"

"Your father may have some good in him," Trunch said, "but I wouldn't lift a finger to help Adam. Even the hogs wouldn't give that skunk houseroom!"

"Well, I hope the worst may be behind us after tonight," Janet Gibson said. "But who can be sure about anything?"

"What have you done, Janet?"

"We sent a servant of Sheila's riding to San Antonio," the dark girl explained. "He was carrying a letter I had penned to the county sheriff. My words informed Risley Hanks of the pass to which Luke Fletcher has brought things here in Miles Grove. I also told Hanks of what had happened to you, and gave the best account I could of the plotting that goes on at the Tumbleweed and the rustling which backs it up. I asked Mr Hanks if he would either come here himself or send a deputy sheriff to supersede Carl Ives's authority and put Fletcher under arrest."

Perplexity wrenched Trunch's features and he whistled doubtfully. "It's all right as far as it goes," he said, "but how far does it go?"

"We've had word from the county sheriff," Janet Gibson hurried on. "It came this evening. Risley Hanks and a party of deputies are spending the night a few miles up the trail — in Batesville. He's asked that we ride out and meet him at eight o'clock tomorrow morning. The meeting will take place where the Batesville trail just misses the eastern corner of my father's ranch. After that we shall inspect the evidence, and the rest will be a matter of riding into Miles Grove and making what show of force is necessary. Sheriff

Ives will know better than to tangle with professional law, and Luke Fletcher will be in for a nasty shock if he tries to resist arrest."

"What did you mean when you spoke of inspecting the evidence?" Trunch asked. "I'm not being pernickety, girl, but this seems to me a bit weak and woolly. If you want it straight, I'm disappointed. This has got to be Wolf Bottoms again. I can't believe that place is still being used as a cache for stolen cows."

"It is," Janet Gibson assured him.

"Where else are those beeves to be put?" Sheila Wilson demanded. "It's not so easy for a rustler to hide the gather when numbers are involved."

"Okay," Trunch said judiciously. "What happens if we're seen heading for Wolf Bottoms? Me and those guys who tried it before ran into a fight."

"This is a different kettle of fish," Sheila Wilson reminded. "We're talking about County law now. Janet wants Risley Hanks to see for himself and

189

accuse her father of being a cow thief. Ben, we all know what that can mean, and Billy Gibson is no hero. He's going to be a man caught between the muck and the sweat — and just right for the offer of a deal. I'm talking about a promise of leniency from the court if he gives evidence for the state." She paused questioningly. "Well?"

"My father," Janet Gibson added, "is the one witness that Fletcher would find impossible to refute. He's a direct accomplice. Anything dad fails to spill, you can be sure Adam will."

"It's too cut-and-dried," Trunch announced objectively. "It depends on everything going right. Things never pan out that sweetly."

"But it could work?" Sheila Wilson said, her voice half questioning and half insistent.

"It's all right in theory," Trunch acknowledged. "Though I don't see a pack of hardcases shunning a fight just because a county sheriff is leading the other side."

"I've said we can't be sure — " Janet Gibson began, breaking off and snatching her head sharply to the left as the barking of a dog outside the front door of the house abruptly caught everybody's attention.

"What's that?" Trunch demanded.

"This is my house," Sheila Wilson replied, "and that's my dog. I left him out on the front step just in case."

"Of what?"

"Fletcher coming this way," Sheila answered. "Old Jack absolutely hates Luke. He lets out when the man is anywhere near."

"That dog's a good judge of character," Trunch allowed. "But what exactly does it mean?"

"I'd say the jailbreak has been discovered," the older woman returned, "but Luke has his doubts that you've fled town. Maybe that sidewinder knows me too well."

"There's no maybe about it," Janet Gibson said tensely. "Neither Ben nor I must be caught here with you!"

Footfalls could now be heard approaching the front door through the increased barking and snarling of the dog; and, after some threatening shouts from the visitors and a loud yelp of pain from the animal, a fist thundered on the front door and the peremptory echoes of the knocking filled the house.

"Get out of here, you two!" Sheila Wilson breathed. "Hide on the lots until they've gone!"

Seizing the dark girl's left hand, Trunch drew her in the direction of the back door.

8

EVERY move had to be made as silently as possible. Trunch breathed at his companion to step lightly. But she was already moving faster and more smoothly than he. Now, breaking free from his grasp, she glided out into the passage and went to the back door, squeezing it open and then gesturing for him to precede her out into the night. He did as Janet Gibson wished and, throwing a swift glance back, saw Sheila Wilson heading in the direction of the hall at a more normal pace. She was humming a tune as she went, and putting on a good act of being alone. Then he and the dark girl were outside and the back door shut in their wake, all sight of Sheila abruptly lost to that inner world which now seemed half a universe away.

Trunch blinked around him. The sudden darkness was something into which he didn't dare plunge recklessly. Even Janet Gibson appeared rooted to the spot, and the only contact between them was the tenuous one of her fingertips resting upon the top of his spine. "It's black as a pit out here!" he muttered, picking up a faint rattling of bolts from the front of the house and an ensuing conflict of voices which was full of hectoring male overtones and shrill female protestations. "There's Sheila going at it! I wonder if those varmints will listen to her?"

"Listen to her!" Janet Gibson softly echoed. "Having come here in these circumstances? Ben!"

Taking her point, Trunch groped towards the back of the lots and, after covering about eighteen paces, sensed the presence of a building directly ahead of him. He heard the heavy movements of stabled horses suddenly disturbed within, and realized that they had reached the structure in which

Sheila Wilson kept her mounts. The immediate temptation was to enter the stables and bolt up behind them, in the hope that the hiding place would prove adequate; but it was all too obvious that the reverse could prove true and the stables receive special attention if the searchers did come back here; so he drew the girl aside, determined to go further afield, and they rounded the left end of the building and he kept veering in that direction, but his companion suddenly plucked at the slack of his shirt and whispered: "It's all rubbish and obstructions that way. We must go behind the stables — still further back."

"What's there?" he inquired tightly, nevertheless swinging in the direction that she wished to go.

The girl didn't reply, but Trunch accepted that Janet Gibson probably knew this ground far better than he and remained compliant, his swiftly improving night sight now providing a faint silhouette of his surroundings and the outline of a large clump of twisted scrub ahead. Judging this to be their destination, he angled his body to the best advantage and slipped into the vegetation's gnarled branches, conscious of a faint rustling in the sparse leaf as his follower joined him, and they came to a halt within the ancient growth and stood quite still while they listened at their wake, heads bowed and not far apart. "I can't believe they'll come this far back," the girl whispered, clearly trying to explain her recent request for their change of direction. "We're not contained either. If we have to make a run for it, there'll be nothing to hinder us."

"No good trapping ourselves between walls at that," Trunch agreed. "Can you hear much?"

"Yes," she replied, "I think they've come through the house. I'm certain now they're going to search out here."

Frowning to himself, Trunch said nothing. His hearing at full stretch, he picked up noises which seemed to confirm what the girl had already reported. He had prayed that the seekers would be satisfied with simply searching through Sheila's house on the off-chance and ignoring the grounds of the property, but there could be no doubt that Luke Fletcher was himself present and that his probable suspicions concerning what had happened after his, Trunch's, escape from the town jail were as strong as his actions seemed purposeful.

Now feet came trampling from the direction of the house, and voices spoke tersely. Trunch formed the impression of a party several strong advancing on the stables and spreading as it came. He saw a gleam of light scything in the blackness as a lantern swung, and swore under his breath, since the likelihood that the searchers would carry lights had somehow escaped his reckoning. His right hand went to his waistband — where he had tucked the revolver which his rescuer had given him — and he drew the weapon and thumbed back its hammer, ready to shoot if the hunt came on as quickly as he now feared and discovery occurred, but a voice that he recognised as Luke Fletcher's abruptly called attention to the presence of the stables and ordered his companions to search there — whereupon the seekers closed on the front of the building, the sound of an opening door was clearly audible, and the light from the lantern vanished as the timbers of the structure blotted it out.

Then, for want of a better expression, Trunch almost jumped out of his skin, for a shape moved sinuously through the growth before him and halted at his feet. A quivering hide then found solace against Trunch's left knee, and he put down a hand and felt the dog's head under his fingers. "Hi, boy!" he murmured, as a soft tongue licked his thumb. "You keep quiet, Jack!"

"Oh, Jack, you old pest!" Janet Gibson protested fondly, kneeling close to the animal and no doubt placing her hands where she could swiftly seize the animal's muzzle should it give any sign of betraying them.

The search of stables went on for about a minute. Men's voices growled in argument, and there was a further bumping and snorting from the disturbed brutes within. Then, with a sense of frustration gathering, Luke Fletcher's voice once more rose above the others, ordering the search of the stables to terminate and extend further afield outside; but then another voice challenged — Ray Porlee's, Trunch thought — and the new speaker said: "We're wasting our time out here, Fletch! It's as black as black hogs, man! Let's wait for the morning! We can put Cherokee Lee, the tracker, to work then on the other side of town! It's the tracks of that horse we need! Once we have those, we can put together a big posse and have us a real ride!"

"You could be right," Fletcher responded uncertainly. "This does have the smack of labour in vain. All right, men. Let's get back to the saloon."

The seekers began to withdraw in the direction of the street. Trunch blew softly through his lips, and heard Janet Gibson release her tension in a low sigh. The dog stirred too, and began to pant. Yet it had all ended in a far less nerve-wearing fashion than might have been expected. Lowering the hammer of his Colt, Trunch thrust the weapon back into his waistband, then fondled old Jack anew. After that, sensing that the girl was about to move, he enjoined a spell of continued caution, for there was no hurry and every reason to let the hunters get well clear.

They gave it another couple of minutes. Hardly a twig stirred, and the stillness of the town was now at one with that of the surrounding countryside. Then the dog whined and broke free of all restraint — giving notice that you could be too careful — and it snaked out of the scrub and made off in the direction of the house.

The girl moved after the animal immediately, and Trunch stepped into the open behind her. He allowed her to lead him back to the rear door of Sheila Wilson's home. The older woman was waiting for them there, with the dog — now revealed as a large black creature, shaggy and crafty-eyed — sitting between her feet and looking up into her face. "So there you are!" Sheila said amusedly. "I began to wonder if you two had eloped or something!"

Trunch smiled faintly. "Just making sure."

"They're long gone," the woman assured him. "But there is no harm in being careful. I was afraid you'd hidden yourselves in the stables, and I almost had apoplexy when I heard Luke and those hellions of his going in there."

"We had more sense than that," Trunch said shortly. "But it sure was a splutter."

"We hid among those old shrubs,"

Janet Gibson put in. "It's very dark, Sheila, and those men weren't all that ambitious."

Sheila Wilson nodded. Then she led them into the kitchen, where she slumped down in a wooden armchair beside the hearth and considered them anew, looking older than her years for the moment and rather drained. "Thank God you're both safe!"

"Speaking of that," Trunch said, "won't your father be wondering where you are, Janet? I gathered you were sort of a fixture in the Broken G ranch house."

"It's all right," the dark girl replied. "It has been my habit for a long time to spend the occasional night in town at Sheila's house. Dad can be a hard taskmaster; but even a worm will turn, and he knows my value too well to try making a prisoner of me."

"I see," Trunch said, seeing very little at all. "Any woman has the right to friendship."

"Listen to that nosey jackass!" Sheila

Wilson jeered. "He can't think how we became pals. Perhaps Janet will tell you about it one of these days, Ben."

"Yes," Janet Gibson said soberly, "perhaps I will — some day."

"Figure they've got me outnumbered, Jack?" Trunch asked the dog, a wry lift to his left eyebrow.

The dog gave its tail a single wag, then turned and walked to a large wicker basket that stood in the corner to the left of the passage door. Jumping into the basket, it turned a couple of circles, fell flat, and shut its eyes, making it plain that it was going to sleep and had no further interest in human affairs. It wished to be disturbed no more.

"He's got the only idea that counts for much at this hour," Sheila Wilsom commented. "Janet and I will be using the two bedrooms I've prepared upstairs, Ben. You can sleep in this chair for tonight. You can stand that, can't you?"

"I could sleep on a bed of nails right

now," he answered.

"I supposed so," Sheila said, rising from her seat and stifling a yawn. "It should be a busy day tomorrow, and I think all's been said that needs saying. Let's go to bed, Janet. Sleep makes us forget our troubles — and that's mighty agreeable." Trunch made an approving sound. He could offer no word against that. And he stood by while the two women left the kitchen, passed through to the hall, then climbed the stairs to the floor above, where they separated and went to their respective rooms, closing the doors behind them. After that he sat down in the wooden armchair and shut his eyes, going off to sleep almost at once, and the early morning light had already paled the flame in the lamp to nothing when he awakened again and heard sounds from above which told him that the women upstairs were out of bed and almost ready to come down again and rejoin him. The night had seemed that short.

Both Sheila Wilson and Janet Gibson

had re-entered the kitchen within ten minutes. Cheeks were pale, eyes heavy, the yawns obvious, and 'good mornings' perfunctory. The older woman got a fire burning and brewed a pot of coffee, while the younger one put bacon and eggs for three in a big steel skillet. She began frying the food as Sheila started pouring the coffee, and Trunch and the older woman watched her at work as they drank. With the frying done, the breakfast was shared out and consumed very promptly. After that Sheila put down a plate of food for the dog, and the utensils were laid aside for later cleansing. Then the three of them — plus their canine companion — left the house and walked down the untended kitchen garden to the stables. Here, in the act of entering, Sheila Wilson glanced round and said: "I've a mount inside that you can use, Ben. I'll bring it out to you."

"Thanks," Trunch said. "I don't suppose you know what became of my own horse. I left it tied up outside the

Tumbleweed saloon — before I rode off on your mare."

"It was taken to the livery barn," Sheila responded from inside the stables. "Carl Ives has been planning to sell it to pay for your funeral."

"That sits well with my breakfast!" Trunch snorted, glaring resentfully as a chuckling Janet Gibson passed into the building to join the older woman. "I bought that damned horse to carry me — not bury me!"

He sensed that the two females were making faces at each other, and was given a few minutes to smoulder over the insensitivity of his friends before Sheila Wilson led a big barrelled dun gelding out to him. She showed him the brute's teeth, put the reins in his hands, and patted the saddle to draw attention to the fact that it was a new one. "There you are, son," she said. "Don't say mother never does anything for you."

"Won't you drop it, Sheila?" Trunch asked acidly. "The horse looks all right, and the saddle will do."

"That gun's pretty good too," the woman persisted, patting the saddleholster as she moved away again. "My very own Winchester Seventy-three. You can knock a flea off old Jack's ear with that. I only hope you won't need to use it."

"So do I," Trunch tossed back, as Sheila re-entered the stables; but, drawing the rifle from its sheath and inspecting its loads and freshly oiled ejector mechanism, he felt intuitively that the day would not end without violence — perhaps a great deal of it — and he knew that much of Sheila's flippancy was an expression of her secret fear; for, when you went up against a villain like Luke Fletcher, you had to accept that there were no holds barred and a woman's life meant exactly the same to him as a man's — nothing!

Janet Gibson emerged from the stables shortly after that. Her right hand was near the bit of a small black mare that walked behind her with a toss of its head and a kick of its rear hooves. It wanted to be off, and the girl talked to it softly as she mounted up — while they both kept a wary eye on old Jack; for the hairy mongrel had the faintly wicked look of a dog that was not above harassing horses when the owners were not around.

Then Sheila reappeared for the second time. She was leading the strawberry mare on which Trunch had seen so much recent action. The horse saw its erstwhile rider standing by, and nickered at him shyly — accepting his slap on the rump in very good part — and Sheila Wilson looked the animal in the eye and said: "You're a flirt, my woman!"

Trunch climbed into his saddle at that, winking at the dark girl as he did so. "Now I wonder," he said innocently, "where she got that from?"

Lifting into her own seat, the older woman quirted her horse into motion. "Come on, you two!" she called back.

"Let's get out there and meet that man Hanks!"

Trunch held back a trifle. He let Janet Gibson move a few yards ahead of him before nudging his own mount to the trot. This left him adequate room to manoeuvre when, as he expected, Sheila Wilson turned left along the top of the lots and rode through the narrow gap between some sour apple trees and the back walls of the properties that formed a masking presence along the northern side of the main street, heading for the town's eastern exit. Riding in the erratic fashion which the sheds, garbage dumps, and fences of the strip forced on them, the three riders soon reached the Miles Grove limits and bent to the right. They came out on the Batesville trail at once, and after that it was just a matter of riding into the pale brightness of the risen sun and starting to add up the miles.

Jack, the dog, was their outrider. He loped this way and that and, though no longer young, seemed to cover the ground effortlessly. Trunch watched the animal, taking pleasure in its joy, and he was of the mind to ask it to bring him one of the jackrabbits which were so plentiful at this hour, when it suddenly checked atop the right-hand wall of the shallow grassy valley through which the trail passed immediately ahead of the riders and, facing east — with its head thrust forward and paw raised like a gundog's — gazed intently across the country beyond which the people on the lower ground could not see.

The animal's pose was too significant to ignore, and Trunch, who had hunted the marshes of the upper Pecos with dogs on many occasions and knew their ways, decided that it would be unwise to travel on without first taking a look at what the dog had seen that he could not; so, without alerting the two women to his intentions, he left the trail on his right and headed up and outwards, arriving on a minor plateau and finding himself with an excellent view of the terrain that was still of such interest to the dog.

Reining in, Trunch lifted in his stirrups and peered towards a landfold about three-quarters of a mile away. He was sure that he detected movement there, and a moment later he made out a party of about a dozen horsemen who were galloping along parallel with the Batesville trail. Wishing that he had his field-glasses to hand, Trunch gave his full attention to the riders, trying to identify one or more of them, but the men were just too far away for their features to be distinguishable. There seemed nothing about the party that was openly threatening, yet he felt instinctively — as had appeared the case with the dog — that there was danger yonder, and Luke Fletcher inevitably came rushing to his mind as the source of it.

Now Trunch kicked his horse to the gallop. Moving swiftly into a curve — which took him to the further edge of the plateau — he achieved a better view of the riders beyond him, and this time he received a strong impression that the lean, straight-backed leader of the party was none other than Ray Porlee, the master gunman in Luke Fletcher's employ. This appeared to confirm his intuitive fear of trouble in the offing, for those men over there could only be shadowing him and the women with a view to scotching their plans — known or only suspected — and they would now have to alter their own actions to match what was happening.

Swinging back towards the trail, Trunch kept his horse going flat out for several hundred yards — believing that his effort on the higher ground would bring him out somewhere near even with the two riders on the lower — but he discovered that, on reaching the western brink of the little plateau, he was still some distance behind the pair beneath, and he was forced to drive his mount still harder, downhill and then up country, before overtaking them. But he was instantly made aware, on rejoining the women, that his absence had not gone unnoticed, for Sheila Wilson turned her face to him and asked: "What is it, Ben?"

"Riders," he informed her, nodding eastwards. "Your dog spotted them. I've got them pegged for Ray Porlee and a bunch of Fletcher's gunhands."

"You are sure about that?" the woman inquired. "This is the time of day when ranchmen ride about in packs."

"I'd put money on it anyhow."

"They're shadowing us?"

"Army fashion, yes," Trunch replied. "Got to be."

"How can that have happened?" Janet Gibson called in dismay. "Our plans were entirely secret, and I'm as sure as anybody can be that nobody saw us leaving town just now."

"She's right!" Sheila Wilson declared, dismissing the shake of Trunch's head. "Everything we've done has been dead secret!"

"Okay," Trunch said. "But it's no good trying to fool ourselves that Fletcher isn't as sharp as we are. A man like him doesn't need a bookful to go on. How many horses do you normally keep in your stables, Sheila?"

"Two, as a rule," the older woman responded. "This mare and a second brute. I see what you're getting at. Luke was in my stables last night. He could have wondered later about the three horses standing there."

"He could have recognised mine," Janet Gibson said. "He has seen it before."

"That wouldn't be enough to act on," Sheila Wilson averred. "No!"

"Then it must have been to do with Martin Loudner," Janet Gibson reflected. "It was him you sent to San Antonio, Sheila. That was around a week ago, and he must have been missed in that time. It's possible Luke linked Martin's reappearance in town with the jailbreak last night."

214

"And worked backwards from it?" Sheila queried. "Luke could have had Martin tipped out of bed and questioned."

"Now that's more like it!" Trunch declared. "It's real frightening to be woken up in the middle of the night and punched around by folk asking questions. You may be sure, if a guy has the information to impart, he's going to spit it out before long."

"Yes, that is perhaps the answer to it," Sheila Wilson conceded. "It isn't all that far-fetched when you come to think about it."

"If it is like that," Trunch reminded — "and I reckon we now have to assume that it is — then Fletcher knows just what we're on this morning. He's aware that we're riding to meet the county sheriff and that he's in deep trouble."

"Risley Hanks and his men are in danger of being ambushed," Janet Gibson observed tensely.

"You've said it!" Trunch agreed.

"Those men yonder would have bushwhacked us first had it been otherwise. It figures they're aiming to catch us all together and kill us in one go!"

"That's my view of it too," Sheila Wilson confessed. "It doesn't matter how you look at it, people are going to get murdered if we don't put a jerk in it!"

"We've got to warn Risley Hanks and company before they ride into trouble," Trunch acknowledged. "Simple as that."

Sheila Wilson's goad thwacked on her mount's rump. Off she went at full gallop, and Trunch and Janet Gibson were immersed in the dust raised by the strawberry mare before they could get going once more.

9

FORGETTING all but the vital needs of the job in hand, Trunch lashed with his reins and gave himself up entirely to the wild dash up country. For a short while he was aware of Janet Gibson's galloping presence at his left shoulder, but then she fell back and he gave her no further thought. The shape of the rider ahead drew him onwards with magnetic force. Yet fast as his own horse travelled, Sheila Wilson's mare went even faster, and the gap between it and his own mount widened by several yards in every hundred. Off to the right, the dog dashed with them, going like a black streak, and the anxiety of it all kept the blood surging in every vein. Faster — they must go faster! This was truly life and death!

A line of low bluffs rose ahead,

and the trail bent across the front of them, tilting slightly uphill and northwards after that. Trunch knew that they had just passed the eastern boundary of Billy Gibson's Broken G range, and prepared to swing into the climb adjacent to the flank of the ranch which Sheila Wilson had already entered. Then he saw smoke puff atop the nearby cliffs and heard a rifle bang. In the same split second, Sheila threw up her arms and toppled sideways out of her saddle, striking the ground with unbroken force and then lying twisted and inert.

Trunch kept riding at top speed. The woman's still figure came closer and closer. Within yards of the fallen Sheila, he was tempted to rein back and spring down; but then the full urgency of their mission imbued him anew and he pulled out around the bleeding shape and continued his gallop northwards, swinging over to his left and making of himself the most difficult target that he could, since he feared that the rifle which had so recently put a bullet in the woman must now be aimed at him.

He heard the explosion. Lead hit his cantle, burying itself deep, and he felt his saddle twist against the belly leathers. The rifle cracked a second time, its echoes giving a quick and angry roll. This slug plucked the band of his trousers, and a third grooved his pommel, burned leather stinking. Now the bushwhacker was pumping his ejection lever hard. The detonations cracked and boomed, and bullets arrived in rapid succession, one passing close to his left shoulder and another cutting a tuft of hair out of his horse's mane.

The tension screwed tighter. Reverberations rumbled and split, reaching the horizons as a collapsing fan of noise. Trunch rode with an almost unbearable pressure in his throat, and his heart was jumping and kicking around in his chest as if it wished to cram a lifetime of beating into what could be his last moments. How much more of this could he survive? Then lead hit a stone beneath his mount's barrel and sprang up at him, just missing his left cheek, and he got the idea that the rifleman had given up on him as the target and was now shooting at the horse itself. This seemed to be confirmed as a bullet clipped the underside of the brute's jaw, causing it to recoil a trifle and veer before recovering itself and racing onwards. A following slug burned the animal's rump, raising blood and, just as Trunch feared that the next shot might do it, the firing ceased — as on an empty magazine — and Trunch once more lifted square to the trail and encouraged his horse by every means. They covered ground freely and, when the rifle spoke again, seconds later, the bullet fell just audibly in his wake and he knew that he was clear of danger for the moment.

The rising trail was now approaching a dull green ridge which was ribbed red with sandstone. Trunch could see the dark V which carried his path across the height, and he kept his eyes upon it, still driving his horse with little mercy. Then he saw shapes emerging from the notch and watched them take on the forms of horsemen — riders who were coming at him almost as fast as he was heading for them — and he was fairly sure that he was looking at the law party from San Antonio which he and the two women had set out to meet.

He went on clattering northwards. The figures ahead took on character and detail in his sight. He perceived that they were all men of a superior cut — well-mounted, well-dressed, and well-armed — and quite soon they met each other over sliding hooves and he was saluting a sandy, long-haired, fox-sharp man who wore a five-pointed star within a circle upon the left breast of his jacket. "Mr Hanks?" Trunch gasped out.

"I'm County Sheriff Hanks," the other agreed curtly. "Who are you?"

"The name's Ben Trunch, Sheriff," his informant responded breathlessly. "You could shortly be under attack, sir."

"Could we now?" Hanks mused, easing his grey Stetson upon his brow and brushing a speck of dust off his corduroy trousers. "So that's what your unseemly haste was all about. At that, we had heard firing out this way and were clapping it on ourselves. I've had a report concerning you. Is Miss Janet Gibson involved in this?"

"And Miss Sheila Wilson too," Trunch replied, twisting round in his saddle and looking back down the trail which ribboned southwards behind him. "They were with me, back there behind the corner. The rifleman you heard sounding off got Sheila with his first bullet. I guess Janet is with Miss Wilson now."

"The shooting was Luke Fletcher's work?"

"On behalf of, Sheriff. Luke speaks for the devil around these parts."

"Didn't I read you were in jail, Trunch?"

"I was, sir — but I'm not now."

Humour glinted momentarily in the county sheriff's frosty eyes. "Fun and games, eh?"

"Some might think so," Trunch allowed, movement at the tail of his right eye drawing his attention into the eastern quadrant, where he saw the body of a horseman whom he had earlier glimpsed at a distance rising from under the nearby land and galloping for the riders halted upon the trail in what could only be full attack. "That's them, Sheriff — the enemy. They're Fletcher's men!"

"Is he with them?"

"I don't believe so."

"Very well," Hanks said shortly. "If there's a battle to be fought, we might as well fight it now. Go for them, men, and shoot to kill!"

Yanking his mount's head round, Trunch drew the revolver from his waistband and kicked his horse into the counter-charge. He rode headlong at the enemy. This was exactly how he liked it. Attack was the only form of defence with which he had ever been happy, and Hanks was the kind of leader who won fights. If he didn't greatly care for Hanks the man, the county sheriff's spirit matched his own, and he could sense the other's fierceness as they rode abreast with pistols cocked and raised.

Flame ribboned opposite and gun-smoke blew. The first volley crackled and popped, a splutter of pyrotechnics in the morning still. Remembering that he had only the cartridges in the cylinder of his Colt with which to make his fight — since a rifle was no weapon for close work — Trunch held his fire and let the parties merge before actually picking a target. Then he singled out a rough-hewn fellow who looked more dangerous than most and put a bullet into his midriff, passing on as the other folded over his pommel and showed no further sign of fight. Coming from the shadow of one victim gave Trunch first chance with another; and that was all he needed, for he scattered his man's brains with a shot fired from almost point-blank range.

It was bloody work, and the firing now intense. Men were going down like ninepins, but Trunch was pretty sure they all belonged to the other side. Firing obliquely, he put a bullet in another man; but then a shot whipped across his nape and had him yelping with fright. Feeling a wave of hatred from the direction in which the slug had come, he let an eye travel quickly towards the source of the shot, and he made out the presence of Ray Porlee through the roiling powdersmoke.

Porlee's gun was pointing again, and his invitation to battle clear; but, short of ducking such a formidable foe, Trunch lifted his horse and sent it plunging towards the infamous gunman. Porlee fired again, and his adversary felt the numbing sting of flesh stripping off a rib as lead creased him.

Trunch straightened his back and took deliberate aim, intending to get Porlee with a single shot, but a horse suddenly bumped his own and he was forced to turn aside without pulling the trigger. Cursing, he kept his bleeding torso on the twist and contrived to keep Porlee clearly in sight.

The gunman had another go at him, triggering a second near miss, but now Trunch was able to hold his aim and let fly in answer. His bullet struck Porlee in the left arm, and the man jerked round in his saddle, shocked by the lead's impact. He was obviously hurt — had indeed turned ashen — but his fury kept his eyes alight and his teeth bared. Thumbing back the hammer of his gun, he aimed with icy care, then spurred in, plainly needing a closer shot. But he delayed that split second too long and Trunch got in ahead of him. This time the bullet hit him in the centre of the breast, and he swung away, spewing blood and trying to keep a grip on his gun, but the weapon exploded suddenly and kicked out of his grasp, falling into the bunch-grass below. He reached after it, trying hard, but sagged ever more deeply over his right knee, and he slowly left his saddle and came to rest on the ground — where a body-length shudder and the drumming of his toes marked the end of his life.

"Ray's down!" somebody yelled. "Ray's dead!"

"To hell with this!" another voice panicked. "Let's beat it!"

Silence came abruptly to the field. It seemed that the fighters on both sides paused to see what would happen next. Attention fixed for a moment on the newly dead Porlee. Then the surviving hardcases — and there weren't so many of them — wheeled their horses away from the lawmen and started galloping off in all directions. It was potentially a rout, and the deputies from San Antonio prepared to give chase, but Risley Hanks stopped all that by yelling: "Hold it, men! We've more to do than chase smallfry!" He glanced across at the slayer of Ray Porlee. "Isn't that right, Trunch?"

"Yes, sir," Trunch answered. "Won't you follow me? I'm off to see how it stands with Sheila Wilson."

"Very well," the county sheriff said, turning this way and that to arrive at a count of his own men, who appeared to have come through the fight entirely unscathed. "Ike Green and Jed Fulcher! Kindly stay here and do what you can for the wounded. The rest of you — come along!"

Trunch had turned his horse and was already on the move. He could hear Hanks and the three deputies galloping directly behind him as he slanted a southerly course back to the trail and then headed for the corner that hid the downed Sheila Wilson from view.

Coming to the bend, he rounded it without any break in pace, then reined in hard and sprang down when he reached the spot where Sheila lay. Janet Gibson was kneeling over her

said evenly. "A comedian I can do without. This does put me in an awkward spot, you know. I've been letting other folk make the running for too long. Even the law can't do just as it pleases. I was relying on a favourable outcome when we left the trail. Now we're simply trespassing. That isn't good or allowable. I ought to be carrying some kind of warrant for what we're about."

"We're here," Trunch said bluntly, "and Janet Gibson is with us. What more do you want?"

"Typical Army man!" Hanks snorted. "Yankee cavalry through and through!"

"He's right, Ben!" the girl called. "Dad will take his belt to me for this!"

"And I'll take mine to him!" Trunch roared angrily. "What's more, I'll kick Adam's fat backside twice round this ranch if he puts his ugly mug in!"

"That's enough, Mr Trunch!" Hanks announced. "I can begin to understand how you've landed in so much trouble.

Discretion isn't exactly your strong point, is it?"

"Sheriff," Trunch answered unrepentantly, "if a thing needs doing, you do it. Yankee cavalry or any other. Everything goes askew while you're waiting on the niceties. If Satan takes advantage of God, that's how he does it best — or so my colonel used to say."

"He could even be right, Trunch — away from civilisation, that is — but here we have to abide by the civil code." Hanks straightened the front of his waistcoat with a hard tug from the bottom. "Enough of this! We *are* here — and cows *do* leave tracks."

"That wasn't what I said," Trunch muttered.

"But that's what you meant, wasn't it?"

"Sort of," Trunch admitted. "You don't see. Around here it's all blamed cattle tracks in the mire!"

"It's his turn to say something right, Sheriff," Janet Gibson said, shaking her head at Hanks. "This land can be almost pure swamp in wet times."

"Give me strength!" Risley Hanks pleaded. "We must do the best we can, and hope that everything turns out all right. No more, please!"

The dark girl gave Trunch a hard, inviting glance.

"Very well, Janet," he said. "I'll show these gentlemen the way."

They had almost ridden across Wolf Bottoms while the talk was going on. Trunch shivered. The low meadows were cold within the shadows of the walls that cupped about them. Kicking his mount, he quickly led the party across what was left of the grass and into the mouth of the tunnel which passed under the ridge and gave access to the Drago swale on the further side. Calling for a dismount, he then led the party through the underground way and out onto the pitted surface of the sunken place beyond. Then, after waiting for his companions to emerge from the tunnel-mouth in his wake, he steered off to the left and called: "See how it is?" Then he concluded the present stage of the ride by leading all concerned up the northern wall of the depression to the dry ground along its rim.

Now they began following the brink of the swampy low in the direction of the not far distant brush and, looking to his left and down, Risley Hanks said: "You could indeed drive a number of cows across that pin-cushion of a valley bottom without leaving any helpful tracks. But it is only a local difficulty. We must ride south, and cast about. If a herd was driven this way, we should find signs of where it emerged."

"That's my idea now," Trunch said. "Trouble is, we're not so far from Billy Gibson's home ground about here."

"We'll soon be in full view from the main work areas of the ranch," Janet Gibson added. "I ought to go home and explain all this to dad."

"You stay where you are, young

lady!" the county sheriff ordered. "You're more help riding with us here!"

They went on moving along the valley brink — in the same unsure manner as before — and, as they neared the eastern corner of the brush and Trunch saw a pair of buzzards flying above, a new thought concerning the thickets came to his mind; but he had no time to develop it, for the approach of many hooves at full gallop became audible from the northeast and the heads of the law riders immediately swung round. "Oh, it's dad and the men!" Janet Gibson exclaimed, uttering a loud groan before adding: "Now we're for it!"

"Halt!" Hanks ordered. "Don't let me see any man here with a gun in his hand! I'll handle this!"

Reins clasped by his fingers, Trunch sat with the palms of his hands resting on the cap of his pommel. He watched the county sheriff move away from the rest of the law party and ride slowly to meet the charging ranchmen, a staying hand raised and his head and shoulders braced authoritatively.

Now Trunch looked beyond Hanks at the oncoming riders from the Broken G ranch area. Billy Gibson was visible at the head of his cowboys, and the giant Adam was lolloping along beside his father on a horse better suited to pulling a cart than carrying a man. Guns were in evidence everywhere among the ranchmen, and Trunch feared that they were going to ignore Risley Hanks' authoritarian signal and simply open fire; but then a pair of sobering shots were blasted into the air from a spot at the edge of the nearby thickets and all eyes turned towards the noise. Movement was already visible amidst the brush, and a body of cattle was driven into the open a moment later by six horsemen. Trunch promptly recognised the riders as Charlie Stokes, lately master of the Rafter S, the four Askews, and Bob Median, one-time boss of the

Toppling M — the fugitives of the thickets and all victims of Luke Fletcher's criminal scheming.

Billy Gibson stared at the figures emerging from the brush, and he brought his riders to a stop with a great shout. His own horse skidded to a halt not seven yards short of where the county sheriff's was placed. For a few seconds longer he gave his main attention to the figures from the thickets, cursing through his teeth, then he bowed his head and became silent, a man clearly striving to accept defeat. But all at once the frustration of it became too much to bear, and he lurched back in his saddle and lifted his right fist, shaking it crazily at the horsemen from the brush. "May you rot in hell!" he screamed. "How could you do it, you lowdown, crawling, stinkin' varmints?"

"It's no good taking on like that, Billy!" Charlie Stokes shouted back. "There's only one of that there breed you're mouthing about present here, and that's you! You're a cow thief, Billy, and some kind of crook after Fletcher's kidney! Ten years ago — nay, five — we'd have found a tree and left you hanging there with a nasty case of croup!"

"You over there!" Risley Hanks raved at Charlie Stokes. "My name is Hanks. I'm the county sheriff from San Antonio. Any more of that lynching talk, sir, and I'll see you go to prison for five years. Do you understand me?"

"Sure!" Stokes responded. "You're a plain spoken man, Mr Hanks. But I've had enough of folk scaring me. You get yourself over here and have a look at these cows. They were brought over from Wolf Bottoms, around sunup, and driven into the brush by some of Billy Gibson's men who also take pay from Luke Fletcher. You'll see as pretty a collection of brands on these critters as you're likely to see anywhere. I reckon Gibson deserves to hang, Sheriff. Whether legal or from a bough would make no difference to me. He'd be just as dead!"

"You savage!" Hanks flung back.

"Only with a cause, Mr Hanks," Stokes retorted, his companions roaring their agreement.

"Billy Gibson and that skunk Fletcher should be done to death this day, Sheriff!" old Jonathan Askew announced defiantly. "That's the truth, sir, and nothing but the truth; and if I have to give an account of those words in court, I'll do it gladly. Fletch is a land-hog, and Gibby is a greedy-guts! They've been out to suck the rest dry for years! You get the full tale of what Fletcher's done about here, and Billy's helped him hide, and you'll have a fair read to take to the privy with you."

"All right!" the county sheriff shouted back. "Be quiet, sir! I don't know your name, but I'll never forget your mouth. Yet I'm glad you're here. There's more to this than I've been able to tell yet.

I'll tell you what I plan, if you'll all keep quiet and give me your attention!"

"What you plan!" Jonathan Askew sniffed. "I've heard about Risley Hanks and his plans!"

"My word is my bond, gentlemen," Hanks said, "and fairness is my pride. Those who do well by me will be done well by." He pointed a finger at the rancher opposite him. "William Gibson!"

"What d'you want, Hanks?"

"Your signed statement that you've been in cahoots with Luke Fletcher of Miles Grove," the lawman replied. "Give me that, with the facts of your involvement — and any other important details of Fletcher's crimes that you know — and I'll do everything I can to keep you out of jail."

"You're offering me a deal?" Gibson asked narrowly, licking his lips, twitching furtive glances around him, and appearing more scared by the moment. "You'll keep me out of prison?"

"*If* it's in my power," Hanks stressed sternly.

"Heed him, dad!" Janet Gibson pleaded. "Trust him!"

"It's your only chance," the county sheriff warned. "Please don't look over your shoulder like that. Fletcher's men are not going to ride to your rescue. We put paid to them a few miles north of here and not so long ago. You may even have heard the gunfire."

"We did, we did," Gibson admitted. "Now ain't that a bitch!" He let out a long sigh, then spat. "All right, Sheriff. There's been shooting enough. Let's ride back to my house and get out the writing things."

"That's wise," Hanks said. "But I'll have to take you in all the same."

"Figures," the rancher acknowledged, gesturing complete surrender.

"Pa!" Adam Gibson wailed in protest, opening his mouth in the matter for the first time. "You can't do — !"

But he got no further in telling his parent what Billy could or could not do, for two rifles spoke a harsher language from back in the brush, and the startled Trunch saw the Gibsons, father and son, come down from their saddles like a pair of felled trees.

10

TRUNCH backed his mount a little. He watched Risley Hanks and Janet Gibson, along with three other people, spring off their horses and run to where the shot pair were lying in the grass. He saw Billy Gibson stir, as hands were laid on him, but the giant Adam remained inert. Knowing all that was possible was being done there, Trunch yanked his horse to the left and rode over to the ground on which the men who had recently emerged from the brush were sitting their mounts about the cows which they had driven into the open. "Who did that?" he demanded, peering anxiously into the thorny shrubs beyond him for fear that the rifles might bang again.

"It could only have been Luke Fletcher and Carl Ives," Charlie Stokes responded. "We spotted them hours ago. They came over to watch these cows being moved. We've had our eyes on them ever since, and been waiting for their next move. It's come, and it looks like they've thrown their hands in."

"It sure does," Trunch agreed. "I doubt there's any way back from what they just did. They must have panicked and gone that step too far. I'm going to ride into the brush after them — right now!"

"Wait along — !" Stokes began.

But Trunch was already on the move. He sent his horse plunging into the thickets, conscious that if he delayed any longer the bushwhackers were going to get completely away. He snaked this way and that, master of the fast, tight ride, yet the chase put no great strain on him, for his knowledge of the brush was again the vital factor. Indeed, the local pattern of the growth made only the one line of retreat sensible, and he pursued this at about three times the pace that men unfamiliar with the ground would be likely to manage.

Yet he also knew that his advantage could not last. There were plenty of points further on where the fugitives could divert and baffle him. Trunch pressed his horse, determined to bring Fletcher and Ives in sight before the thickets swallowed them completely, and he zigged and zagged amidst the tangles of juniper, mesquite, live-oak and cacti, left ear tilted and a watchful eye sweeping the breaks among the screening growth ahead, and presently an eruption of birds near a knot of aged vegetation — slightly to his right and no more than a hundred yards before him — betrayed the presence of his quarry in a fleeting glimpse of two hat crowns.

Then, as if some malign spirit meant to promise only to deceive, his progress was checked where he entered brush that was unexpectedly dense. All at once he felt cut off and alone, and it would have been easy to become disorientated, but he hung on to his wits and kept his senses straight, soon emerging from the dusty obscurity of the hanging bean bunches to a view of rising ground amidst the thickets of the nearer scene.

With the morning light now at its clearest, Trunch studied the crest of the low, stone-littered ridge that crossed his line of vision just above the height of the tallest of the shrubs in his path. He recognised the formation, and knew there was a sheer drop of about thirty feet beyond it. According to his judgment, on the earlier clues, Fletcher and Ives were heading for the crest — and the retreat that it would force on them. Then he saw them, riding up the slope within a short space of where he expected them to be, and he made a quick shift to his left, hoping to place himself directly in line with their inevitable withdrawal from the ridge.

What Trunch had foreseen was precisely fulfilled. The two fugitives,

lighter man's face, shoved him back, kicking at the same moment with his right foot.

Trunch felt the kick land on his ribs, exactly where Ray Porlee's bullet had raked him. The agony of it sliced through his body like a blade and, as the blood flew, he heard himself shriek out. He also found himself cartwheeling across the clearing, and he came to rest on his back just short of his erect but dazed-looking horse. Braced on his elbows, he gazed at Ives through a teeming vertigo, terrified lest the other charge and trample him; but the big fellow still seemed mainly intent on getting away, and he returned to his horse — which had now steadied down a bit — and this time he managed to heave into his saddle without too much difficulty.

Out of the clearing he galloped, and that should have been the end of it; but suddenly — indeed irrationally — he reined in at the edge of a thicket and wheeled his horse round to face his enemy again. Nudging the brute towards the rigid Trunch, Ives reached for the rifle in his saddleboot. Jerking the Winchester, he levered at its magazine and lifted a cartridge into the barrel. Then he put the rifle to his shoulder and aimed at his downed foe. Coming sharply back to life, Trunch did the only thing he could and flipped into a backward somersault, passing under the barrel of his mount as the big lawman's slug tore into the earth which he had covered the instant before.

Climbing to his feet — mind and senses still spaced out by faintness — Trunch perceived that he was standing next to the rifle scabbard on his horse, and he snatched the Winchester out of leather and pumped its ejection lever faster than the mounted sheriff could manage. He fired on the split second, taking no aim, and his bullet clipped Ives's left cheek, opening up a nasty wound there and causing the sheriff to jerk round and blaze his second shot yards wide of its mark.

Cocking his rifle again, Trunch got a firm grip on himself and, resting the barrel of his gun across his saddle, took careful aim on this occasion and shot the crooked lawman through the body. After that he pumped two more bullets into the centre of Carl Ives's breast — the giant shuddering visibly each time he absorbed lead — and the light of life slowly faded from Ives's eyes and he toppled limply towards the gun that had delivered his death wounds, hitting the ground face first. His right boot remained loosely caught in its stirrup, and this seemed to irritate his horse, for the brute gave a sudden chuck forward and caused the foot to thud to rest, the whole seeming to round off an action that had been nicely executed.

Tipping the Winchester across his shoulder, Trunch stepped round his horse and went to where the felled giant lay. He gave Ives a kick, knowing there would be no response, then went to Luke Fletcher's sprawling figure and did the same, again bringing out no twitch. He had done well. As ever, he had kept his nerve and shot straight. Yet, no matter what the evil of the men he slew, no man could take pleasure in killing — and it was as much in sadness as relief that he turned away from the corpses and watched riders come breasting out of the nearby thickets, an olive-skinned deputy sheriff from San Antonio at their head. "You haven't left a whole lot for us!" the deputy observed, eyeing the bodies as he reined in.

"No?" Trunch queried, smiling bleakly. "Well, you're welcome to whatever there is."

"Hanks isn't very pleased with you, boy."

"My fight," Trunch retorted, "first and last. What do you guys know anyhow?"

"We do our job, and draw our pay."

"Where have I heard that before?" Trunch sighed. "What about Billy Gibson and that son of his?"

"Gibson is sore hurt," the deputy answered, "but he ought to make it. His son is dead."

"No loss there, believe me."

"The girl seemed real worried about you," the deputy remarked, his smile a questioning one. "There was a little talk back there, and I reckon that, with Luke Fletcher now dead — that is him yonder, ain't it? — his land-grabbing is all bust out. Did I hear the next ranch yonder is yours?"

"On what you suggest, could be."

"Well, that Gibson ranch sure is nice," the deputy commented, "and it'd be a sight better with another married up to it."

"Get out of here!" Trunch scorned, touching the blood that was trickling down his side. "Hell if I'm good for much now but the butcher's yard!"

"Aw, you'll mend," the deputy said indifferently. "You don't look like a dier to me!"

Maybe not. Trunch walked slowly back towards his horse. He believed that kick from Ives had broken a couple of his ribs. Anyhow, he wouldn't be riding back to Fort Sumner this month. New Mexico and the Army would have to wait. For quite a while perhaps; and by then, a new state of mind could have taken over from the old. Being a civilian had its compensations; and Janet Gibson could be one of them. A woman's smile settled so much in this life. He'd leave it at that for now.

THE END

FIGHTING RAMROD
Charles N. Heckelmann

Most men would have cut their losses, but Frazer counted the bullets in his guns and said he'd soak the range in blood before he'd give up another inch of what was his.

LONE GUN
Eric Allen

Smoke Blackbird had been away too long. The Lequires had seized the Blackbird farm, forcing the Indians and settlers off, and no one seemed willing to fight! He had to fight alone.

THE THIRD RIDER
Barry Cord

Mel Rawlins wasn't going to let anything stand in his way. His father was murdered, his two brothers gone. Now Mel rode for vengeance.

ARIZONA DRIFTERS
W. C. Tuttle

When drifting Dutton and Lonnie Steelman decide to become partners they find that they have a common enemy in the formidable Thurston brothers.

TOMBSTONE
Matt Braun

Wells Fargo paid Luke Starbuck to outgun the silver-thieving stagecoach gang at Tombstone. Before long Luke can see the only thing bearing fruit in this eldorado will be the gallows tree.

HIGH BORDER RIDERS
Lee Floren

Buckshot McKee and Tortilla Joe cut the trail of a border tough who was running Mexican beef into Texas. They stopped the smuggler in his tracks.

BRETT RANDALL, GAMBLER
E. B. Mann

Larry Day had the choice of running away from the law or of assuming a dead man's place. No matter what he decided he was bound to end up dead.

THE GUNSHARP
William R. Cox

The Eggerleys weren't very smart. They trained their sights on Will Carney and Arizona's biggest blood bath began.

THE DEPUTY OF SAN RIANO
Lawrence A. Keating and
Al. P. Nelson

When a man fell dead from his horse, Ed Grant was spotted riding away from the scene. The deputy sheriff rode out after him and came up against everything from gunfire to dynamite.

FARGO: MASSACRE RIVER
John Benteen

The ambushers up ahead had now blocked the road. Fargo's convoy was a jumble, a perfect target for the insurgents' weapons!

SUNDANCE: DEATH IN THE LAVA
John Benteen

The Modoc's captured the wagon train and its cargo of gold. But now the halfbreed they called Sundance was going after it . . .

HARSH RECKONING
Phil Ketchum

Five years of keeping himself alive in a brutal prison had made Brand tough and careless about who he gunned down . . .

FARGO: PANAMA GOLD
John Benteen

With foreign money behind him, Buckner was going to destroy the Panama Canal before it could be completed. Fargo's job was to stop Buckner.

FARGO:
THE SHARPSHOOTERS
John Benteen

The Canfield clan, thirty strong were raising hell in Texas. Fargo was tough enough to hold his own against the whole clan.

PISTOL LAW
Paul Evan Lehman

Lance Jones came back to Mustang for just one thing — revenge! Revenge on the people who had him thrown in jail.

HELL RIDERS
Steve Mensing

Wade Walker's kid brother, Duane, was locked up in the Silver City jail facing a rope at dawn. Wade was a ruthless outlaw, but he was smart, and he had vowed to have his brother out of jail before morning!

DESERT OF THE DAMNED
Nelson Nye

The law was after him for the murder of a marshal — a murder he didn't commit. Breen was after him for revenge — and Breen wouldn't stop at anything . . . blackmail, a frameup . . . or murder.

DAY OF THE COMANCHEROS
Steven C. Lawrence

Their very name struck terror into men's hearts — the Comancheros, a savage army of cutthroats who swept across Texas, leaving behind a bloodstained trail of robbery and murder.

SUNDANCE: SILENT ENEMY
John Benteen

A lone crazed Cheyenne was on a personal war path. They needed to pit one man against one crazed Indian. That man was Sundance.

LASSITER
Jack Slade

Lassiter wasn't the kind of man to listen to reason. Cross him once and he'll hold a grudge for years to come — if he let you live that long.

LAST STAGE TO GOMORRAH
Barry Cord

Jeff Carter, tough ex-riverboat gambler, now had himself a horse ranch that kept him free from gunfights and card games. Until Sturvesant of Wells Fargo showed up.